"You've been ~~very~~ ~~~~ ~~~~ ~~~~ is said, his voice dropping, "but I don't expect you to talk to me in public. I understand how it is. I promise it won't hurt my feelings if you blow me off."

Zoey hesitated. What was she going to do about this? It seemed awfully hypocritical to talk to Lucas here, even to enjoy talking to him, and then pretend that she couldn't stand him later.

Lucas grinned crookedly. It was meant to look tough and indifferent, but the corner of his mouth collapsed a little. "I'm a big boy," Lucas said. "I can handle it."

"No one can handle it," Zoey said. "You can't live life totally cut off."

Suddenly she stopped. She had reached for him without thinking. Her hand, dripping with sugar glaze from the sweet roll, was covering his. Slowly Lucas's fingers entwined around hers. Neither of them was breathing. Zoey's heart was beating so loudly she was sure he could hear it.

"I . . . I got you all sticky," Zoey said, her voice a squeaky gasp.

Lucas raised their locked hands to his lips. He brought her sugary index finger to his mouth. His eyes were nearly closed, his every movement in slow motion.

Look for the other books in this romantic series,
coming soon from HarperPaperbacks

And don't miss Katherine Applegate's
Ocean City series

*coming in July

BOYFRIENDS
GIRLFRIENDS

ZOEY FOOLS AROUND

KATHERINE APPLEGATE

HarperPaperbacks
A Division of HarperCollins*Publishers*

To Michael

Grateful acknowledgment is made for permission to reprint a quotation from *The Big Sleep* by Raymond Chandler, Vintage Knopf. Copyright © 1939 by Raymond Chandler. Reprinted by permission.

HarperPaperbacks   *A Division of* HarperCollins*Publishers*
            10 East 53rd Street, New York, N.Y. 10022

Produced by Daniel Weiss Associates, Inc., 33 West 17th Street, New York, New York 10011.

First printing: February, 1994

Printed in the United States of America

HarperPaperbacks and colophon are trademarks of HarperCollins*Publishers*

10 9 8 7 6 5 4 3 2 1

Zoey Passmore

Here's the question: Love. What is it? Absolute and unshakable? Eternal and undying? Faithful and true?

Oh, really?

Have you ever been to a dance? Ever seen the way a guy will look right over his girlfriend's shoulder while he's slow dancing with her and give some other girl the eye?

Ever kind of thought about your boyfriend's best friend, or even his brother? Don't lie. You know you have.

So what's love? Something that lasts a week or a month and that's all you can expect? Or is it just that some loves have a short shelf life? You know, like yogurt: after a week or two they go bad.

And how do you recognize the other kind of love, the kind that isn't like yogurt? The kind that's more like . . . I don't know, like peanut butter, that lasts forever and always tastes good?

Okay, maybe not peanut butter. But you get the idea.

So, getting back to the point, what's love? I guess no one can ever be totally sure, and after all, I am just seventeen. Cut me some slack; I can't be expected to know everything. I finally understand the War of 1812, and that's hard enough without having to worry about defining love in a hundred words or less.

Still, I have learned some things about love, especially lately. And I know a lot more about it now than I did, say . . .

. . . two years ago.

Two Years Ago

"Jake. Jake. Jake! Would you . . . would you stop it? Jake, I'm serious. Look, stop it, get your hands . . . I'm getting pissed off now. I'm serious; stop it right now." Zoey Passmore slapped her boyfriend's hand away, a startlingly loud sound that made several passersby turn and stare in amusement.

"Jeez," Jake said, looking wounded and rubbing the back of his hand.

"It's my ice cream. You ate yours and you've already eaten half of mine." She held it up as evidence. "I'm down to the waffle. You pig."

"The waffle?"

"You know, the waffle cone. What do you call it?"

"The cone," he said, shrugging his big shoulders and staring at her as if she'd said something utterly idiotic.

"What? What are you staring at me for?"

"It's not called the waffle. It's the cone. Ice cream cone." He shook his head. "Man, you think you know somebody."

4

"Well, I'm a complex, mysterious woman." She licked a big dollop of the chocolate ice cream.

"That's so sexy the way you do that," Jake said.

"Oh, shut up." She glanced around self-consciously, wondering if anyone else had heard him. The crowd on the narrow, cobblestoned street was mostly tourists, people in big, bright shorts and golf shirts, old people and couples dragging small children through the souvenir and fudge shops that lined Exchange Street. Still, here and there were familiar faces, some of Chatham Island's three hundred full-time residents.

"Sorry," Jake said without any hint of remorse. "I'm just feeling good today."

Zoey softened, letting a smile form on her lips. It had been two months since Jake had felt good. "What do you want to do today?"

He leered comically, an expression that seemed out of place on his serious face. "Same thing I want to do every day."

Zoey sighed. Yes, Jake was getting back to normal, for better or worse. "Okay, if you want to go watch sports on TV . . ."

"You know what I meant."

"Yes, but I'm ignoring you." She dodged around a stroller and rejoined him, reaching for his hand. "Why are you feeling good today, anyway?"

Instantly his innocent, happy expression

5

changed. His smile grew cold. "Today's the day Lucas goes off to jail."

She felt her own face stiffen. "Are you sure?"

He nodded. "Of course I'm sure. I thought we might get lucky and run into him. I'd enjoy seeing him go. Just like I'll enjoy thinking of him locked up."

Zoey released her grip on his hand. "You shouldn't talk that way," she said softly.

"Why not? He deserves it. He killed my brother."

"I just don't think it's right. What happened to Wade was terrible, but still, what's happening to Lucas isn't something to be happy about."

"Is to me," he said darkly.

A cute ten-year-old girl came running up, a tornado of knobby knees and silken brown hair. "Jake!" she yelled.

"Hi, Holly," Zoey said.

"Jake, Dad said you're supposed to help him take Mr. Geiger's boat out of the water."

"Oh, crap. I forgot." Jake winced and looked at Zoey apologetically. "I told my dad I'd help out down at the marina today."

"Great, so you just eat my ice cream and take off?" Zoey asked.

Jake leaned close and kissed her lightly on the mouth. "I knew you'd understand. Sorry. But come over tonight, okay?"

"I'll check my calender," Zoey called after his retreating back.

She wandered on through the crowd, feeling the sunshine of the brief Maine summer on her shoulders. This strange, tragic summer was finally close to an end.

She walked past all the familiar shops, following the gentle downhill slope toward the dock. There, in the wider spaces, the crowd was less dense. She could see a line in front of her parents' restaurant and hesitated, unsure what to do. If she went anywhere near the place, she'd get drafted into working. Of course, she could use the money. Sophomore year was about to start, and she needed to replace her now dorky freshman clothes.

But it was just too nice a day to bus tables.

She ate some more of her ice cream, biting off chunks of waffle. Yes, waffle, she thought defiantly.

The crowd opened up suddenly, and to her surprise she found herself staring at a guy, standing alone, leaning against a pole by the ferry gate. His blond hair tossed and fretted in the breeze. There were people all around, but it seemed as if a force field surrounded him, leaving him utterly separate and apart.

Lucas.

The image leapt at her, a picture of loneliness. He was gazing with sad, despairing eyes at the

7

bright town, seeking to memorize every image, seeking to hold on.

The ferry whistle shrieked and she saw him flinch, a strange and telling action. No islander raised to the sound of that whistle ever reacted. Yet Lucas had flinched as if he'd been stung.

Were his eyes filled with tears? She couldn't be sure from this distance. Was he searching the crowd for a particular face, hoping that someone, anyone, would come to say good-bye?

A false hope. No one on Chatham Island would break the isolation that had been imposed on the boy who'd brought tragedy to the island. His father, hard-faced and grim, stood on the bow of the ferry, waiting to escort his son.

Zoey eased closer, moving in dreamlike slowness. Lucas's gaze at last focused on her, his attempt at a smile crumbling, his attempt to hide his tears failing, too.

"Hi, Lucas," she said, lowering her eyes to the ground.

"Hey, Zoey," he said without expression.

She stood there, an arm's length away, not knowing what else to say. He said nothing, only brushed surreptitiously at his eyes. She stared at the remnants of her ice cream cone. Then she looked up.

She had never looked into sadder eyes.

She reached out with her free hand and gripped

his arm. "Look, take care of yourself, okay?"

Lucas looked as if her kind words might destroy his last reserves of control. He nodded.

Zoey started to turn away, but some unseen force stopped her. She stepped forward, paused, then with infinite gentleness kissed his lips.

He stared at her uncomprehendingly.

She gulped hard, flustered and amazed at what she'd done.

"I . . . I just thought someone should say good-bye."

The ferry whistle shrieked again. The final warning.

"I have to go," he said.

"I know," she answered.

"Thank you," he said.

"Here." She held out the last of her ice cream cone. "You may not get any ice cream for a while. . . ."

He smiled sadly as he accepted her gift. "I guess not."

"There's not much left," she apologized.

He stared at her long and hard. She felt his eyes move from her long yellow braid, to her bare, tanned bare arms, to her freckled nose . . . and settle on her eyes.

"That's okay. The waffle's my favorite part," he said before he turned away.

9

Youth Dies in Drunk Driving Accident

BY LISA SOO

Special to the Weymouth Times

CHATHAM ISLAND—In many ways it is becoming all too common a story. On the evening of June 27, tragedy touched the lives of three Chatham Island youths, leaving one dead, one injured, and one, apparently, directly responsible.

Wade McRoyan, 18, was killed when the car he was in struck a tree along Coast Road on Chatham Island. A second passenger, Claire Geiger, 15, suffered a mild concussion and a broken wrist, along with contusions and abrasions. Ms. Geiger is the daughter of Burke Geiger, president of Mid-Maine Bank of Weymouth. The third occupant of the car, Lucas Cabral, 16, was uninjured. Police say Cabral was able to pull the injured parties from the car and seek assistance.

Police also say Mr. Cabral has admitted to being the driver of the car. The officer on the scene administered a Breathalyzer test, which showed Cabral to be legally intoxicated. Ms. Geiger was tested at Weymouth hospital, and the deceased was later tested by the medical examiner. Both were found to have blood alcohol levels well above the legal limit for adults.

Continued on Page A2

Continued From Page A1

This is not the first such accident to occur in the greater Weymouth area, but it has hit especially hard in the small Chatham Island community of 300 permanent residents. There has never been a fatal automobile accident on the island, which has few roads.

Police will bring charges of drunken driving and vehicular manslaughter against Lucas Cabral. Contacted by telephone, Cabral refused comment.

Burke Geiger stated that his daughter is in good condition and is not expected to suffer permanent injury. "She's going to be fine, thank God," he said. "This whole thing is such an utterly senseless tragedy. My heart goes out to the McRoyans, whom I know well. I can only imagine the pain they must be feeling."

As to the accused Lucas Cabral, Geiger would only say, "I hope that young man will learn from this very sad episode."

One

"Five days, five lousy days. Not a month or several months or a year, no, not even a full week. Five days." Nina Geiger drew deeply on her cigarette and exhaled clear, pure Maine sea air. "Five. Tomorrow it will be down to four. The next day—"

"I'm guessing three?" Zoey said.

"Two."

"One."

"Then . . ."

"Blastoff?" Zoey suggested.

"School," Nina said, crumpling the unlit cigarette in her hand and tossing it toward the trash can. She was allergic to smoke, but the cigarette went with a certain image she liked, so she smoked without lighting. The cigarette missed the trash and landed on the chipped gray-painted steel deck of the ferry. The bay breeze blew it in little circles.

"Better get that. Skipper Too will throw you overboard for messing up his boat," Zoey said.

Skipper Too, who was really named Tom Clement, was the captain of the *Minnow,* which was actually called the *Island Breeze. Gilligan's Island* reruns were always popular on the island.

Nina looked defiant for a moment, then leaned forward to retrieve the cigarette. She was wearing black fishnet stockings, thigh-highs that were artfully ripped in several places. Over them she wore baggy army shorts. She had on a brown leather jacket that clashed with her black Doc Marten boots.

"So you're looking forward to school?" Zoey asked, deliberately provocative.

"Just like I look forward to my period every month. Like I look forward to going to the dentist to have my molars drilled." Nina pulled a second cigarette from her pack of Lucky Strikes and popped it in the corner of her darkly lip-sticked mouth.

Zoey waited. There was bound to be a third example.

"Like I look forward to finding out the milk has gone sour after I've already taken a swallow."

"The three-part comic tautology rule," Zoey said.

"You remember that?"

"Nina's First Rule," Zoey said. "Funny examples work best in threes."

"Going from least funny to most funny,"

Nina added. She sighed. "At least you're going to be a senior."

"Yeah, you'll just be a lowly junior. Whereas I will have all the glory and power associated with being a senior." She shot her friend a sidelong look.

The breeze freshened, caught the bow spray, and flung it against Zoey in a fine, cold mist. She grimaced and zipped up the front of her red fleece L.L. Bean jacket. She wore khaki shorts, white running shoes, and a white cotton blouse. It was just right for the warm day ashore in Weymouth, but the twenty-five-minute ferry ride to Chatham Island always had the potential to grow cold, even on a bright, late summer day.

She bent over to rummage in her ferry bag, a stretch net affair that no islander would dream of traveling without. It was loaded with college-ruled notebook paper, yellow plastic pencils, soft-grip pens, a three-ring binder decorated with abstract pink triangular designs, and a new ribbon for her typewriter. It also held the items that had been on her father's list: a dozen bulbs of garlic, an annoyingly heavy bag of eggplant, and a glass jar of saffron. Finally, concealed beneath everything else, Zoey found the cookies.

"Want one?" she asked.

"What are they?"

"Fig Newtons."

"Fig Newtons suck."

Zoey glared at Nina. "Five more days," she said. "And by the way, junior girls play a lot of basketball."

Nina shivered. "Don't be cruel just because I don't like your taste in cookies."

"Lots of dribbling and running." Zoey opened the cookies and popped one in her mouth. "Basketball separates the dorks from the near-dorks."

"At least I won't be the one showering with Claire," Nina said slyly, reaching into Zoey's bag for a Fig Newton. "She separates the melons from the lemons."

"I don't let your sister bother me anymore," Zoey said. "It's stupid to be annoyed at someone just because they have a perfect body and once compared you to the Great Plains. While doing an oral report in front of the class."

"That was years ago," Nina said. "You're not the Great Plains anymore. Of course, you're not the Rocky Mountains, either."

"Jake thinks I'm perfect," Zoey said. She looked ahead toward Chatham Island, drawing closer now. From this point, she knew it would take exactly six minutes to round the breakwater, slow down into the enclosed harbor, sidle up to the town dock, and tie off the ferry. She'd taken the trip a few million times during her

15

ten years on the island. She also knew that as they rounded the breakwater she'd be able to look up the ridge and see Jake's house. He might even be on the balcony, using his dad's telescope to watch them come in.

"You know, these aren't horrible," Nina said thoughtfully as she chewed on a cookie. "You just have to get past the fact that they're all mushy. I like crisp."

The ferry rounded the concrete breakwater and brought the island's only town into view across the calm, gray water. North Harbor was a cluster of red brick, painted wood, and weathered gray-shingle buildings. Shabby-looking wooden lobster traps piled five deep lined the docks around several high-bowed, rough-looking fishing boats with names like *Santo Cristo* and *Santa Maria*.

The highest point in the town was the needle-sharp church spire. But behind the town, the green and pine-wooded ridge rose higher still, forming a barrier to the growth of North Harbor. A few buildings peered out through the trees on the slope, quaint inns that catered to the warm weather tourists.

"Why exactly do you hate school, anyway?" Zoey asked. "When we were little, you liked it better than I did."

Nina sucked on her unlit cigarette. "I was

young and unformed then. That was before I realized that school is specifically designed to crush the spirits of people like me."

"It's designed to crush everyone's spirits, Nina. Don't take it so personally. I told Mrs. Bonnard—you'll have her this year for English—I told her I wanted to write romance novels when I grew up, and she said the people who wrote those kinds of things were literary whores. I had to use a bicycle pump to reinflate my dreams."

Nina smiled. "Better to be a literary whore than a literal whore."

"Oh, that's deep. Tell that to Mrs. Bonnard when you see her. You didn't think the bicycle-pump line was funny?"

"I smiled. What am I supposed to do, laugh till I pee?"

Zocy looked up the east slope of the ridge and made out Jake's cedar-sided house. Sure enough, there was a tiny figure standing on the balcony outside his parents' bedroom, no bigger than a fly from this distance. Zoey fought a sudden impulse to aim a rude gesture in his direction. Which would have been inexcusable, she knew. It was just that sometimes it got on her nerves, thinking how ever present Jake could be in her life.

Most of the time, though, it was nice knowing he was always there for her.

She grimaced, confused by the contradiction. Well, consistency was the hobgoblin of little minds. Someone famous had said that. Someone famous who knew what a hobgoblin was.

She let her gaze travel left. She could barely make out the brass weather vane her father had put on their house. Just a few yards up the slope something caught her eye. A guy, far too distant to recognize, standing on the Cabrals' deck.

She glanced at the dock. No, Mr. Cabral's boat was still out at sea. So who was that on the deck? She felt a shiver skate down her spine. Not Lucas. It couldn't be. Lucas was in jail. Or Youth Authority, or whatever they called it.

The thought touched her with gloom. It had been some time since she'd thought of Lucas Cabral. His was not a name that came up very often. Unconsciously she touched her lips, remembering that single, strange, inexplicable kiss almost two years ago. Then she thrust the memory out of her mind.

She looked back at the Cabral house, but the light had shifted just enough so that the deck was hidden in glare. Well, it was probably nothing, anyway.

Zoey said a casual good-bye to Nina at the dock. Nina's house was at the northern end of town, overlooking the lighthouse.

Zoey turned right and crossed the paved open square that served as a parking and dropoff area for the ferry and McRoyans' Marina. It was mostly empty, dotted here and there with island cars—rusted, pathetic wrecks without license plates. North Harbor was only six or eight blocks long, and all of Chatham Island was no more than three miles long, with roads over less than half of that, so people didn't see much need for expensive luxury cars. Real cars were kept on the mainland in a covered lot for trips to the mall, south to Portland, or even to Boston.

Passmores', her parents' restaurant, was only a few feet away, facing Dock Street. Its tiny, three-table outdoor café had one table occupied. She went down the alley to the back door, pausing to stick the lid onto an overflowing trash bin.

The door was open, and she stepped into the cramped stainless-steel kitchen area. A large aluminum stock pot bubbled on the stove, and the dishwasher roared, sending up clouds of steam.

Her father had his back to the door, his hair tied back in a ponytail. He was chopping parsley in quick, decisive strokes, pausing every now and again to shovel the parsley into a pile and take a swallow from a sweating bottle of beer.

"Hey, Dad," Zoey called out.

Her father half turned to look at her. The front of his white apron was stained green and brown. He wore wooden clogs on his feet and a Grateful Dead T-shirt. The mocking, laughing blue eyes were the model for her own. People who saw them together always pointed it out, though the rest of her, the unruly blond hair, the smile that rose more on one side than the other, even the ears that seemed to stick out just a little, were straight from her mother.

"You get my eggplant?" her father asked.

She held up her ferry bag as evidence and began to empty it on the counter. "These were the smallest they had."

"They'll do. You hungry?"

"No thanks," Zoey said. "I ate some cookies on the boat. Is Mom here yet?"

Her father stopped chopping and wiped off the knives. "Yeah, we're both stuck here tonight. Christopher had something or other to do, so I gave him the night off. Your mom's in front, but I wouldn't go out there unless you want to get roped into stocking the bar. Plus she's pissed at me, so she's in a bad mood."

"Thanks for the warning. What are you guys fighting about?"

"I have no idea. She said something about getting fat, I said no, you're not, aside from your butt maybe, you're the same as you always were, and suddenly she's mad. You're a woman, why don't you explain it?"

Zoey shook her head. "I think I'll stay out of it. I guess I'm going over to Jake's house, if you guys are going to be here."

Her father eyed her pile of school supplies. "So, are you looking forward to starting school again?"

"Kind of," Zoey said. "I mean, I'll be a senior."

"Well, you're lucky. I hated school myself. About the only part I liked was cutting classes to go get stoned with my friends." He winced in embarrassment. "You don't do stuff like that, do you?"

"This isn't the sixties anymore, Dad."

"Seventies. Give me a break. I'm not that old." He gave her a comically menacing look. "I could still send you out to count bottles with your mom."

Zoey went over and gave him a quick peck on his stubbled cheek. He smelled of fresh parsley and beer. "I'm out of here."

She walked along Dock Street, swinging her much lighter ferry bag. To her right was Town Beach, a narrow strand dotted with driftwood and seaweed that the tourists avoided, preferring the broader beaches along the western shore of the island.

It wasn't yet five o'clock, Zoey realized, but the sun was already weakening, sliding down toward the low brown-and-gray skyline of Weymouth and turning it into a flat, dark cutout.

No wonder Nina was feeling that sense of impending doom—the days were already growing shorter. Soon the daily routine would involve freezing, predawn ferry rides to school, huddling below in boots and parkas and earmuffs. And return trips in the afternoon would take place with blazing sunsets at their backs.

The island seemed unnaturally quiet, as it often did after a trip to Weymouth. Weymouth was a busy little city, full of rattling delivery vans and gasping buses, music escaping from shop doors and car windows. North Harbor, by contrast, was a place of long silences, broken occasionally by barking dogs, screeching gulls, and the many soft sounds of the water.

Across the harbor, through the masts of the sailboats in the marina, Zoey saw the ferry pulling away, heading toward the two outer islands, Penobscot and Allworthy.

How many trips had she taken on that ferry? Thousands? Tens of thousands? No, not ten thousand. Not that many. Of course, if she lived out the rest of her life here, then it would pass ten thousand eventually.

Not that that was going to happen. She was going to college in California, either UCLA or USC or UC San Diego. Anything involving the letter *C*. She planned to apply to all three and she'd probably be accepted at all three, if she could get the loans and grants worked out.

UCLA would be perfect. Year-round sun, year-round warmth, everybody in convertibles. Lined winter jeans that made you look ten pounds heavier would be a thing of the past. She'd go to classes all week, go to Disneyland or the beach on the weekends. Get a tan. Get two tans. Meet some guy who looked like Marky Mark, only nicer. Fall totally in love and end up having to write Jake a terribly sad letter telling him it was over.

"My dearest Jake," she said aloud to an audience of gulls perched on the seawall. "My darling Jake. Dearest Jake. Dear Jake. Jake. I would do anything to avoid writing you this letter, because I know it will cause you great pain, and that is the last thing I want. You have always been kind and honorable with me, and I know your fondest hope has been that we would wed. Alas, that is not to be.

"Alas?" Zoey laughed out loud. "Right. Try *sadly*. Sadly. Yes. Sadly, Jake, that is not to be. Who can predict the human heart? Who knew I would meet Dirk, the youngest of the Baldwin brothers, while in Hollywood? Who could have foreseen that we would fall deeply, hopelessly in love? Who could have guessed that our wedding would be invaded by photographers from the *National Enquirer*?

"Who knew I would suffer from strange delusions about Hollywood boy toys?" she asked herself. "Who knew I'd end up talking to myself?"

A vehicle rattled down the road, a familiar rust-red pickup truck. It braked beside her and Jake stuck his head out of the window. "Hey, babe. I spotted you on the boat with Ninny."

Zoey crossed over and kissed him quickly on the lips. "Funny, I was just thinking about you."

"I'm always thinking about you. Jump in."

Zoey went around, reached through the passenger side window, and used the interior handle to open the door. The outside handle didn't work. She climbed up onto the high bench seat. Jake kissed her again, longer this time. He had great lips for kissing, Zoey had decided. Not too full, but not thin, either. And whenever he kissed her, even if it was just a peck on the cheek, he always closed his dark gray eyes slowly, as if he were falling into a dream. And, of course, he had a major bod, too, all Solo-flexed and tan, with tic-tac-toe abs and a hard rear that made watching him at football practice a major spectator sport.

Not that Zoey cared much about such superficial things.

His only possible failing was that he wore his dark brown hair fairly short. She would have

24

liked to be able to run her fingers through it.

"Where are we going?" Zoey asked. "I was heading to your house."

Jake shrugged. "I've been home all day. I'm tired of home. I thought we could drive down island and watch the sunset."

"You mean park and make out?"

He grinned. "If we go to my house, my mom will force you to help her make dinner. She's making that scallop thing and those apple things for dessert."

"If I wanted to cook, I could have stayed and helped my dad," Zoey said. "On the other hand, your mom makes great apple things."

"Your dad's still down at the restaurant?" Jake asked.

Zoey made a face. She hadn't meant to mention that. "Yes. That Christopher guy bailed."

"So you're saying there are no parental units at your house?" Jake asked. "It's all ours?"

"Benjamin's home," Zoey pointed out.

"His room's downstairs," Jake argued.

"He has supernatural hearing," Zoey said.

"Right. Just because he's blind does not mean he has any better hearing than anyone else. He told me so."

"That's just what he wants you to believe."

"So we'll be quiet."

"Jake, is making out all you ever think of?"

"No. I also think about what should come next, after making out."

Zoey sighed. "You need to broaden your horizons."

"You're right," he said testily. "And I'd like to broaden them with you. I mean, Zo, we've been going out for three, almost four years. We'll be seniors this year."

"I suddenly have a great desire to be home, watching TV by myself," Zoey said. She opened the truck door.

"Oh, come on, Zo," Jake complained. "Peace. All right?"

Zoey closed the door again. "Okay. Let's go to my house and watch some tube or something." She shot him a sarcastic look. "I think Oprah's doing 'Guys Who Think of Nothing But Sex.'"

Zoey

My romantic life started when I was just thirteen years old. At the time I had long, knobby legs, no chest at all, and stringy blond hair done in a style so awful I've tried to destroy every last photograph ever taken of me in those days. Oh, sure, a person with a keen eye and unusual perception might have looked at me and thought, Well, there's potential there somewhere. But I'm telling you, when I would just stand there in front of the full-length mirror in my bedroom, stand there in all my pink, well-scrubbed glory, the image

that always came to my mind
was of a stick figure. Stick
body. Stick arms. Stick legs.
A circle for a head. A circle
with bad hair.

Jake was my pal in those
days. We'd known each other
since I moved to the island
with my family back when I
was seven. We used to play
catch, Jake and me, with my
best friend, Nina, looking
on disapprovingly. And
we'd hike up the ridge. And
we'd, all of us, Jake and me
and everyone, take the ferry
into town and buy ice cream
and hang at the mall and
just generally waste time.

I thought about boys in
those days, sure. But I
guess it didn't really occur
to me that Jake was a boy.
Jake was Jake. So you see, it
came as a major surprise to
me. We were walking up the

trail along the ridge one afternoon, the whole gang. Jake and I were well out in front of the others, so we stopped to wait for them by a stream flowing with melting snow. I bent over to take a drink, and when I straightened back up, he kissed me. Kind of clumsy, kind of hurried, and we both blushed and looked away and were glad when the others caught up.

Jake's been my boyfriend since that day. Everyone says we're great together, the perfect couple, and I guess we are. He's a very nice guy. The kind of guy whose arms, wrapped tight around you, make you feel small and protected.

And I really like his parents.

Two

"Benjamin? Are you home?" Zoey knocked lightly on the door to her brother's room.

"Yeah. Come in."

Zoey opened the door and stepped inside. Her brother was sitting in gloom, his feet propped up on his antique rolltop desk, his fingers tracing the tiny bumps of a Braille book. Zoey reached automatically for the light switch. Benjamin turned to look back over his shoulder, aiming his sunglasses in her direction. He had worked hard to maintain the habit of looking at the person he was speaking to.

"Jake with you?"

"He's in the family room, channel surfing."

Benjamin nodded. "What's up with you?"

"Dad's working the dinner shift tonight," Zoey said.

"Yeah, I know. Nina's coming over later to read for me. She just called." He reached with perfect precision for one of the built-in shelves of his desk and pulled out a book. He held it up backward for her to see.

Zoey sighed. This was one of Benjamin's running jokes. Like the way he'd decorated his room with maps and posters but had turned half of them upside down. He lived for the times when someone new visited the house and he could point to some upside-down poster of kittens playing with yarn and go on proudly about how much he loved that particular Matisse print. It was a test of character, he said. People who got the joke were all right. People who froze up or played along out of pity were hopeless.

Benjamin laughed and turned the book so she could read the cover. *The Plague,* by Albert Camus. "It's on the suggested list for this year."

"Great," Zoey said. "Nina was already depressed on the boat. That should send her over the edge."

"Nina is always depressed," Benjamin said. "It comes from living in the same house with Claire."

Zoey shook her head. "No one's forcing you to go out with Claire."

Benjamin shrugged. "I hear she's great looking. And she has a nice speaking voice."

Zoey turned off the light and went back out into the front entryway, then down the hall to the family room. Jake was sprawled on the shabby brown couch, a throw pillow under his head, watching *A Current Affair.* When he saw her, he muted the TV. "Hi. How's Benjamin?"

"Nina's coming over in a little while to read to him," Zoey said.

Jake groaned. "Great. Your brother and Ninny. So much for time alone."

"You shouldn't call her that. She's my best friend."

"How about when she calls me *Joke*?"

Zoey sat on the couch. Jake put his head in her lap and she stroked his cheek, looking down at him affectionately. "That's different. You're just my boyfriend."

"I think she started it," Jake said. "Back when I was in, like, fourth grade. She was in third."

"Since fourth grade. You ever think maybe we're all falling into a rut here?" Zoey said.

Jake looked up at her. "Me and Ninny?"

"All of us. You, me, Benjamin, Nina, Aisha. Even Claire. My parents, your parents."

"See? This is the way you get when you've been talking to Nina. That's why I rag on her. She has the power to destroy a romantic mood from clear across town."

"It's not Nina. It's just this feeling of things going on the same way forever and ever."

"You have the end-of-summer blues, that's all." Jake raised the volume on the TV.

Zoey pushed his head off her lap and stood up. She walked over to the window restlessly and looked out at the backyard. It was already growing dark. She stood watching as the color faded from the daylilies in the failing light.

The backyard ended in scrub brush at the base of the ridge. The ridge rose sharply from that point, broken granite boulders and gnarled, stubby trees brightened in the warm seasons by dustings of wildflowers. A few houses were propped on the slope where Climbing Way began its ascent along the ridge. Lights were flickering on in their windows, and curtains were being drawn.

She looked up toward the Cabral home, just above hers on the ridge, remembering the impression she'd had on the ferry that someone was up there.

A movement in the shadow caught her eye. She stared. A dark figure stood there, leaning against the railing, his face red and shadowed in the slanting rays of the setting sun.

"Oh, my God," Zoey said, pulling back from the window. She felt her heart pounding.

"What?" Jake asked, looking at her upside down from the couch.

"There's someone up at the Cabrals' house." Zoey pressed her hand over her heart. "I think it may be Lucas."

Jake froze for a moment, then with sudden speed and grace he was beside her. He leaned against the window and looked up the hill, his eyes intense. "I can't see him very clearly."

"It's probably just someone visiting them."

The figure on the deck moved, and for a moment he was clearly outlined in profile before turning away and disappearing.

Jake stepped away from the window. His lips were drawn back in a snarl. There was an ugly light in his eyes. "It's him. It's Lucas. He's back."

Claire Geiger paced slowly around the rails of the widow's walk, pausing from time to time to look in one direction or another before resuming her regular pacing.

The night was cool, and where she was, high atop the three-story house, the breeze was stiff, bringing with it the smells of salt and seaweed and, occasionally, the faint but unmistakable scents of the roses and fringed gentians in the garden below.

Down in the front yard she could make out a shadowy shape closing the gate and trotting toward the front door. Her sister, Nina.

As Claire leaned over the railing to call down to her, she heard the front door close. Too late. She stayed there for a moment, leaning out into space, her long black hair falling forward, before pulling back.

The rail was just barely waist high, and she sometimes worried that she might fall off, sliding helplessly down the pitched roof, careening between the dormered windows and landing on the hard ground below. Sometimes she wondered if those sorts of worries were secret hopes.

The lighthouse, a squat whitewashed tower on a granite islet, blinked and swept its beam over the corrugated black water. Warmer lights from the rooms below spilled out into the front yard, casting shadows among the bushes and trees. As she paced left, she saw the blinking light on the end of the breakwater, the harsh blue-white lights at the ferry landing, the pinpoints of light shining from the portholes of the boats in the marina. Beyond that were the brighter lights of Weymouth, projecting rippling beams and reflections on the mirror of water. Streetlights blazed, car headlights winked and disappeared.

Another quarter turn and she was gazing out over the town proper, dozens of lights in curtained windows, a green warning light atop the church steeple, floating, disconnected lights poking through the trees on the ridge.

She wasn't sure if she had always been so fascinated by light. She suspected it had begun when she started going out with Benjamin. Being around a blind person made you think about being blind yourself, and somehow that made every color seem more vivid, every light seem brighter.

Right at her feet, a square of buttery light suddenly appeared. Nina's face stared up at her from Claire's room below.

"You up there?" Nina called out.

"Yes," Claire said.

"You coming down?"

"I wasn't planning on it. Not just yet."

Nina climbed the ladder, but kept her head below the opening. She had a fear of heights, at least of wide-open areas like the widow's walk.

Claire stood looking down at her sister's up-turned face, so like her own—the same wide Geiger mouth they'd inherited from their father—and yet unique. Nina's eyes were gray, laughing eyes, one just slightly out of alignment in a way that gave her a look of perpetual skepticism. Claire's own eyes were dark within dark.

"How's the weather out there?"

"Didn't you just come in?" Claire asked. "It's the same weather up here as it is down on the street."

"I know. I was being droll."

Claire nodded. Nina found it hysterical that Claire was interested in weather and planned to be a climatologist someday. "It's getting chilly. Some high cirrus clouds to the south. You want the barometer reading?"

"Cirrus? Are you sure they're *cirrus* clouds?" Nina asked mockingly.

Claire pulled her hands up into the loose sleeves of her baggy sweater and decided to let the remark pass. "So, where have you been?"

"I was supposed to be reading some novel to your boyfriend, Benjamin."

"Don't call him my boyfriend. We just go out sometimes. What do you mean *supposed* to be reading?"

Nina gave her a meaningful look. "Reality suddenly got more interesting than fiction."

Claire inhaled the crisp air deeply. "Are you going to explain, or am I supposed to guess?"

"Think good old days."

Claire sighed.

"Now think bad old days," Nina said.

"Nina, you just keep getting stranger. Or are you just getting more droll?"

"Both. Thanks. That's a cool thing to say." Nina met her gaze for just a second. "Lucas is back."

Claire felt her heart miss several beats. She reached for the nearest railing and gripped it tightly. "Are you sure?"

"Zoey and Jake said it was him, up at his mom and dad's house, hanging around the deck, looking Lucas-like."

"Jake saw him?" Claire asked sharply. "What did he do?"

"Nothing. Yet," Nina said. "But he was definitely wired. It was a very tense scene. Jake took off right after I showed up. Zoey was halfway thinking we should go and warn Lucas. Benjamin talked her out of it, though. He said he didn't think Jake would really do anything."

"Warn Lucas?" Claire bit her lip. "I don't waste a lot of sympathy on Lucas Cabral."

"He used to be your one true love," Nina said provocatively.

"That was a long time ago."

"Two years."

"I didn't think he'd have the nerve to come back to the island," Claire said. She looked toward the south, toward the few wan lights at the base of the ridge. One of those lights must be the Cabral house. One of those lights might be his window. He might be gazing out at this very moment, searching for her with his coolly penetrating gaze. She turned away.

Nina shrugged as well as she could while still gripping the ladder. "Where else is he going to go? I guess he's done his time, as they say. Paid his dues. Made his amends to society."

Claire rubbed her right wrist. A bump on the head and a broken wrist, that's all she'd gotten from Lucas Cabral. The wrist still ached when the weather grew cold and damp.

Wade McRoyan, Jake's brother, had died.

Claire shivered, suddenly penetrated by the cool breeze. Something deep inside her had awakened at the mention of Lucas's name. Anger, an urgent, demanding anger. And fear? No. Why should she be afraid?

"I wonder if he'll be going to school," Nina said.

"I doubt he'll stay on the island for long," Claire replied. "I doubt he'll feel very welcome here."

Claire Geiger

I had just turned fifteen. Sweet fifteen? Maybe. I don't know if I was ever sweet anything. I guess I wouldn't have been in the car if I were all that sweet.

And I was in the car, that much I can be sure of. And I guess I'd been drinking, too, just like Wade and Lucas. Beer that Wade had somehow gotten hold of. We had driven down Coast Road, past the end of the paved part onto the rutted dirt road that winds back into the woods, with trees closing in all around and deer leaping into our headlights to stare.

We were feeling pretty cool. Lucas

and I grabbed a couple of the beers and went deeper into the woods, intoxicated as much by each other as by the alcohol. We were massively in love. I'd have done anything for him, and I believe he'd have died for me if I'd asked him.

Wade stayed by the car, kicking back and listening to the stereo. He'd just broken up with a girl from the mainland and was a little bummed.

I guess Lucas and I made out for a while in the woods. I guess we eventually came back and collected Wade and drove back toward town. I say I guess because I don't remember exactly. I've tried, and sometimes in a dream, or in one of those strange moments of clarity that come when you see a certain picture, smell a certain fragrance that triggers memory, I'll . . . but then it's gone.

I do know what happened later. I know they took me to the hospital with a concussion and a broken wrist. I know that Wade died. And I know that my heart broke when Lucas admitted that he had been the one driving.

Jake came to see me in the hospital. His eyes were empty, his voice barely audible. I told him how guilty I felt. He told me, No, Claire. Lucas was driving the car. Lucas had rammed that tree. Lucas had killed his brother. Lucas was guilty.

And what was I? Just another one of his victims.

Three

The curtains were open and the light was on in Jake's room. Zoey stepped onto the patio and pressed her face against the sliding glass door, searching the room for him. Not on the Soloflex machine. Not sitting at his computer. Not watching his TV.

She tried the door, but it was locked. He was probably upstairs with his parents. Zoey shrugged philosophically. She didn't really want to walk in on the whole family at this late hour, but she felt she needed to see Jake. It had been several hours since they had seen Lucas from her family room window, time enough for Jake to calm down a little, to mellow, as he sometimes did, from anger to his own brand of silent grief and remorse.

She walked up and around the house, arriving at the front door. She knocked, and in seconds Mrs. McRoyan opened the door and squealed her usual enthusiastic welcome.

"Is Jake home?" Zoey asked. "I didn't see him downstairs."

43

Mrs. McRoyan made a puzzled face, wrinkling her blue eyes. "Should be. I can't imagine he'd go out this late."

A sudden worry flashed through Zoey's mind. Had Jake gone off looking for trouble with Lucas?

"I know it's late, but do you mind if I go see if he's down there?" Zoey asked.

"What late?" Mrs. McRoyan protested. "I only wish you'd been here earlier. I had out the trusty Betty Crocker cookbook and was working on the apple tarte Tatin, only this time I was making my own puff pastry. Would you like a piece?"

"Sounds great—like everything you make, Mrs. McRoyan. But I'm kind of full."

"When are you going to start calling me Daisy?" She ushered Zoey inside.

"Oh, probably not till I'm at least thirty," Zoey said. "I think I'll just run on down—"

"Well, you know the way. But if you have time, stop back up here. No one around here appreciates the labor that goes into puff pastry. Sure, they'll eat it, but my husband and Jake and Holly don't understand."

Zoey trotted down the stairs. The rec room light was off, but the door to Jake's room was open. With a sense of foreboding, Zoey hurried forward.

Just then, the door to Jake's bathroom opened

44

wide. Steam billowed out. She turned and saw him facing the mirror over the sink, his face covered in shaving cream.

His face was the only thing covered.

He turned and saw her. His eyes opened wide.

"*Oh oh oh*, I . . . I . . ." she replied.

He slammed the door shut.

She dived toward his room. "Sorry!" she yelled.

"I just shaved my right cheek down to the bone!" he complained, his voice muffled by the door.

"I said I was sorry." She chewed on her thumb. "I . . . I didn't see anything."

"What is that, an insult?"

"That's not funny, Jake," she chided. She heard him laughing softly.

"Look, all I have in here is a towel. Bring me some clothes."

"What?" she asked, looking around at the room and not seeing anything that might be clothing.

"In my closet, on the hook. I think there's a pair of sweatpants."

She found them, a gray pair with *Harvard* embroidered down the leg. She tapped on his bathroom door. "Here."

He opened the door a crack. A hand emerged and disappeared with the pants. Seconds later he came out, holding a wad of toilet paper to his right cheek.

"I just wanted to make sure you were all right," Zoey said lamely.

"I'm not a Ken doll, if that's what you wanted to know."

"You know what I meant."

"Sure," he said breezily. "I'm bleeding profusely and I'm embarrassed. On the other hand, I had been feeling kind of sleepy and now I'm wide awake. Jeez, I just saw *Psycho* on TV last night. You know, butcher knives flashing in the shower? It's amazing how high you can jump when you get that shot of adrenaline. Coach should have seen me."

He pulled the tissue away from his face.

"I think you'll live," Zoey said.

"I don't know . . ."

She put her arms around his broad bare shoulders, her hands barely meeting in back. "You want me to kiss it and make it better?"

"Actually, yes."

They ended up on his bed, making out. After a while they ended up lying together, Jake with his back against the wall, Zoey reclining against his chest, enjoying the rise and fall of his breathing, listening to the deep rumble of his laugh as they watched Letterman together.

At last, as she felt sleep closing in, Zoey got

up, stretched, and headed for the sliding glass door. He followed her, peering out at the night over her shoulder.

"Thanks for coming over," he said.

"I just wanted to, you know, make sure you're okay," she said.

He smiled gently. "I am now, Zo. To tell you the truth, I was pretty keyed up before, but then, you always have been able to make me feel great, just by being around."

She nodded, touched by his emotional admission, so unusual for Jake. "You know what?" she asked. "You do the same for me."

He grinned mischievously. "You could spend the night . . ."

Zoey shook her head tolerantly and sighed. "Good night, Jake."

Zoey woke and lay in bed, listening to the music of her clock radio and warming to the fading tendrils of a dream about Jake. It was eight o'clock, earlier than she had been getting up, but she was trying to get herself back on a school-year schedule. Once school started, she would have to be down at the dock by seven forty.

As she closed her eyes again, a thought was prickling the back of her mind, demanding to be remembered. Oh, yeah. Lucas.

She snapped off the radio and climbed out of bed, twisting her Boston Bruins T-shirt around so that the logo once again faced the right way. Her room had two windows, one on the side that gave a view of the house next door and, if she craned her neck, a sliver of the Cabrals' deck.

No sign of Lucas. Maybe he wasn't even home. Maybe.

She moved to the second deep, dormered window where she had a built-in desk. She leaned across the cluttered desk and drew aside the curtains. The house was perched at the dead end of Camden Street, giving her a view straight down the entire five-block length of the street.

Gentle morning sunlight lit the brick and wood buildings on the left side of the street, leaving the other side in cool shadow. As usual, there was little traffic, only the occasional bicycle, the infrequent island car rattling to or from the ferry. Two blocks down, where Camden crossed the cobblestones of Exchange Street, the old woman who ran the antique store was sweeping the sidewalk in front of her building.

Zoey drew her gaze away from the window and stared at the sides of the dormer. The walls were plastered with Post-it notes—lists and reminders and appointments on the right, quotations on the left. Her current favorite was a quote from Joseph Joubert:

> Imagination is
> the eye of the
> soul.

She had no idea who Joseph Joubert was, but she liked the quote just the same.

Below that was another.

> or a woman
> A man ^can stand
> almost anything
> except a succession
> of ordinary days.

Goethe had said that, and it had been bothering her ever since she'd found it in a book and duly written it down on the yellow Post-it note. Maybe that was why she'd been feeling restless. Maybe her life was becoming a succession of ordinary days.

She showered and shaved her legs and put on white shorts and a short-sleeve blue-and-white-striped top. Her mother was downstairs in the kitchen with Benjamin. She was wearing a bathrobe, her faded blond hair tousled, reading the newspaper and sipping coffee. Benjamin was making himself a bowl of cereal, keeping his thumb hooked inside the bowl so he'd know when he'd added enough milk. Her father would already be down at the restaurant, cooking for the fishermen and the early morning ferry crowd.

"Good morning, everyone," Zoey said cheerfully.

Her mother looked up from her paper and smiled wanly. "Don't be so cheerful; my head can't take it."

"Hung over," Benjamin said, walking with his cereal to the table.

"No, smart guy," their mother said. "I just didn't get much sleep last night." She grinned. "Your father and I were arguing, so naturally we had to make up."

Zoey shook her head and reached for the box of muffins on the counter. "Mom, do you think you could spare us the details? We *are* your kids."

Her mother shrugged. "You do know the facts of life, don't you? I mean, you do know where you and Benjamin came from and all?"

"Yes, of course I know. I just don't need to think about it. You're warping me."

"I don't do all that parental crap, you know that," her mother said, waving her hand dismissively. "You want Donna Reed, go hang out with Daisy McRoyan. She likes to stay home and bake pies while her husband's out banging everything in a skirt."

Zoey glared at her mother. "I don't think you should go around saying things like that. What if Jake was over here and heard you say that about his dad?"

"If Jake doesn't know it, he's the only one," her mother said. She rolled her eyes. "Look, I'm sorry. I take it back. Fred McRoyan's a saint. Everybody on this island's a saint. We're all just one big, happy family." She turned the page of the newspaper.

"I'm going out," Zoey said.

"You going over?" Benjamin asked.

"No, I was just going to head down to the circle, see if anyone's around. See if Nina wants to do anything. You want to come? Or did you want me to pick something up for you on the mainland?"

"Nope. Just wondering," Benjamin said. "Take it easy."

"We could use a few hours of your time down at the restaurant later," her mother said. "Just this afternoon."

"No prob," Zoey said. The restaurant was the whole family's responsibility. Besides, her parents paid her for her work.

"Hey," her mother said suddenly, looking up from her paper. "What's this I hear about the Cabral kid coming back?"

Zoey turned. "We thought we saw him yesterday evening. No one's totally sure, though."

"He was a cute kid," her mother said. "Remember how he'd come down the hill in the morning and bring us those sweet rolls his mom made? Now there's a woman who should open a bakery. Your dad's been after her recipe for years."

"I remember," Zoey said. Lucas would sit at the table and drink coffee with milk before walking with Zoey and Benjamin down to the ferry, where they would meet Nina and Claire and Aisha and Jake. And Wade.

No doubt Lucas would be the subject of conversation on the island for some time.

At least for a while, the succession of days wouldn't be quite so ordinary.

Four

Claire knew they would be there. They were there many mornings, and today, with word of new developments spreading, no one would miss circling.

The circle was at the center of North Harbor, a cobblestoned hub from which five tiny streets spread out like spokes. On one side, the church seemed to stare across the circle and down Exchange to the ferry landing. Around the circle were little souvenir shops, craft galleries, and candy stores that sold fudge to the tourists. On the exterior wall of the insignificant town hall was a compass rose that showed how far it was from Chatham Island to all sorts of cities and locations around the world—845 miles to Bermuda, 1,325 miles to Sarasota, Florida, 14,678 miles to Tahiti, if you wanted to take the long way around.

In the center of the circle was a grassy lawn dotted with a few trees, a couple of quaint, green-painted benches, and a low granite obelisk with a brass plaque bearing the names of the island's war dead since the Civil War. There were nine names altogether, with spare room for more.

Zoey was standing, and Claire's sister, Nina, lounged on a bench beside Aisha, who was trying to catch her mass of springy black curls with a rubber band. Jake leaned against the monument, his head bowed, his big shoulders hunched forward. The usual crowd. Sometimes Benjamin would be there, too. Lately the black guy, Christopher, had dropped by from time to time, obviously not sure whether he was being invited to join the group or not. Hopefully he understood, having seen Aisha, that he wasn't being given the cold shoulder because of his race. It was just that he'd only been on the island since spring.

To Claire's surprise, the conversation was not about Lucas.

"We're the last of a dying breed," Aisha was saying. "I'm graduating this year, Zoey and Ben are both graduating, Claire's graduating."

"Joke will graduate if he can ever get those multiplication tables down," Nina said.

"Chew me, Ninny," Jake said.

"Next year there's not going to be much of an island group at the school," Aisha continued. "Just Nina and my little brother. It will be a few years before Jake's little sister is old enough."

"Kalif's going to the high school next year?"

Zoey asked. "I don't know why, but he never seems that old to me."

"Nina and Kalif, that's it. That will be it for is- islanders." Aisha nodded in agreement with herself.

"You figure one of us should volunteer to flunk so we can keep up the islander tradition at Weymouth High?" Claire asked.

"Would you mind?" Aisha said with her worldly-wise, impertinent grin. "I'd do it, but my folks would be pissed."

"Benjamin would be glad if you flunked, Zoey," Jake said.

"He would not," Zoey said. "Benjamin's not like that."

"Not consciously, maybe," Jake persisted. "But he's not thrilled to be in the same grade with his sister who's a year younger than he is."

"Benjamin's realistic," Claire said. "He lost almost two years being sick and going through rehab. He's already made up half that time." Jake moved away from the monument, and Claire took his place. He had left the granite just slightly warm with his body heat. Or maybe that was her imagination.

"The only bummer is I'll have to ride the ferry alone," Nina said.

"Kalif will be there," Claire pointed out. "Maybe he likes older—stranger—women."

"Are we doing anything today?" Zoey

asked, sounding suddenly frustrated.

Aisha shrugged. "I have to help my mom get the rooms ready. We're booked for the weekend."

"I thought about taking the boat out, maybe do the barbecue thing up at the pond if anyone's up for it," Jake said. He looked questioningly at Zoey, then shot a glance at Claire.

"Just so I know," Claire said, turning to meet Jake's gaze, "since I got here last and all. Did you already deal with the question of Lucas, or are we going to pretend he doesn't exist?"

Jake's expression turned instantly stony. Zoey looked relieved.

"I don't know what there is to talk about," Jake said, almost daring anyone to say anything else.

Claire rolled her eyes. "This is Chatham Island, not Manhattan Island," she said. "It's not like Lucas is going to be invisible. We're going to be running into him, don't you think?"

Jake kicked at a tuft of grass. "This is such crap," he said. "This shouldn't be happening. I mean, what the hell does he think he's doing, coming back here? What does he think we're going to do? As far as I'm concerned, two lousy years in juvy is nothing."

"They gave him the maximum for a juvenile," Zoey said quietly.

"Only because he already had a record," Jake

said. "I don't think the judge gave a damn that my brother—" He lost his voice for a moment, and Claire looked away. "He didn't care that Wade was dead. I mean, if Lucas hadn't had a record, the judge probably would have let him off with a reprimand."

"That's not true," Zoey said, but Claire could see that Jake was beyond listening.

"Vehicular manslaughter," Jake said, sneering at the words. "You get faced and you go tearing down Coast Road in the middle of the night . . . It's not like it's an accident. I mean, it's not like you have to be a genius to figure out that you can't drive stinking drunk without someone getting hurt. His lawyer made it sound like it was all just this unfortunate accident. Son of a bitch should have gone to prison, not juvy. See how big a man he is in prison. See how he likes that."

Jake seemed to run out of steam. He slumped down on the grass, resting his elbows on his knees and holding his head in both hands. Claire had heard it all before. They'd all heard it before.

"We all miss Wade," Aisha said at last, breaking the silence.

Claire nodded. She rubbed her wrist. It had been in a cast for two months. The doctor said her being drunk might have accounted for the mildness of her injuries. Evidently it was better to feel relaxed when you stopped very suddenly.

Except that theory hadn't worked for Wade.

Lucas had been unhurt.

"So what do we do?" Zoey asked.

"Well, it's not like we can get revenge," Aisha said firmly. "If that's what you're thinking, Jake, then stop thinking it."

Jake shook his head. "I'm not going to touch him. My dad said we're just going to have to live with it. He says he thinks Mr. Cabral will get rid of Lucas eventually."

"His own dad is going to kick him out?" Nina asked skeptically. "I don't think so."

"Mr. Cabral is a proud guy," Jake said. "You know how these old Portuguese fishermen are. Son or not, Lucas humiliated him. My dad thinks sooner or later the old man will force him out."

"Jeez, that's cold, isn't it?" Nina said.

"Cold is what he deserves," Jake said sharply. "You weren't hurt, all right, Ninny? I was. Wade was my brother. And your sister was hurt, too. Don't tell either of us about what's cold."

"All right, get a grip," Nina said. She made a face but fell silent.

"If Jake's dad is right, then I think we should help Mr. Cabral . . . deal with Lucas," Claire said.

"How is that?" Jake asked.

Claire met his eyes. "I think we should make sure he knows he's not wanted by any of us, either," she said slowly. "Cut him off totally."

"There's something about this that makes me uncomfortable," Aisha said. "I mean, I don't know—"

"Look, no one's forcing you to do anything," Claire said reasonably. "But we've always stuck together."

Nina shook her head. "Maybe we should just go all out," she said. "You know, grab our pitchforks, light some torches, and march on up the hill and drive the monster out like the peasants in a Frankenstein movie."

"Let's save that for later," Claire said. She looked around the group and saw them nodding, one by one—Aisha troubled, Nina mocking, Zoey almost distracted. Jake deadly serious.

Claire took a deep breath and let it out slowly. For the first time since Nina had brought her the news, she felt . . . relief.

Yes, that was the emotion, she realized. Relief. But why?

Aisha Gray was still troubled when she left the group at the circle and headed toward home.

She was halfway down Center before she realized that she was going to be passing right by Lucas's house on the way to her own. Avoiding it would mean going some distance out of her way and making a much steeper climb. She didn't feel like doing that. The walk back home was steep enough.

So what did they all expect her to do if she went walking past the Cabrals' and Lucas happened to be out front? Was she supposed to ignore him, refuse to answer if he said hello?

It was ridiculous. Jake, she could understand. Maybe even Claire. But why on earth would Zoey go along with this primitive reaction? Just because she was Jake's girlfriend?

The road beneath her feet began to steepen and she leaned into it, stretching her calf muscles, pumping her arms.

There it was, right above the Passmores' house, the little gray shingle cottage with the deck that looked down the hillside. She stole a glance at it. The windows weren't curtained, but the interior was dark. Still, he could be in there, watching her walk past.

She barely remembered Lucas. She'd only come to the island a year before Lucas had left. Mostly she recalled an image of long, unruly blond hair and a face too sweet for the eyes.

She passed the house and kept climbing, feeling a mixture of relief and resentment. This island solidarity crap could get to be too much. On the other hand . . .

Her parents had moved to Chatham Island and bought the inn three years ago, just as she was starting high school. It had been a shaky time for her, moving from Boston to this tiny, lily-white enclave. None of the kids her age had bothered even to say hello, and she'd assumed with sinking heart that it was racism on their part. Maybe to some extent it was.

But when she'd taken the ferry to the mainland that first day, there'd been some subtle change. A couple of the kids at Weymouth High had started in with crude remarks about her race. Zoey had told them to stop, but they had persisted. Which was when Zoey had gone to get Jake and his big brother, Wade. Jake and Wade had made it clear that Aisha was one of them. They didn't even know her name, but what had mattered was that she was an islander.

Of course, it had still taken a year before she'd been really accepted on the island itself. And that's when the accident happened, and Lucas was sent away.

Climbing Way turned and brought Gray House into view. It was a two-story brick structure with an attic ringed with dormered windows. The Gray family, Aisha, Kalif, and their parents, lived in bits and pieces of the huge old mansion. The family room, her parents' bedroom, and the small private kitchen and bathroom were built over what had once, long ago, been stables, a wing of the main house. Aisha's bedroom was downstairs, hidden away. The rest of the downstairs—formal dining room, living room, breakfast room, main kitchen, and foyer—were all stunningly decorated in colonial style, like something straight out of a magazine. Upstairs were the three rooms that were rented out, two smaller rooms and a truly magnificent room called the Governor's Room that had a private bath with a huge whirlpool.

It was a lot like living in a museum.

Someone was sitting on her front porch. It wasn't hard to figure out who. Aside from her own family, there was only one other African-American on Chatham Island. This particular one was holding a handful of wildflowers.

Christopher stood as he caught sight of her. "Hi. I was waiting for you. I figured you were down at the circle with your friends."

Aisha nodded. "Uh-huh."

"Here, these are for you." He held the flowers toward her.

"They are?"

"Sure. I picked them in the yard of my apartment building. The landlady said it was okay as long as I . . ." He stammered to a halt. Then he recovered himself. "As long as I was going to give them to a young lady."

Aisha looked from the flowers to his face and back again. He had shrewd brown eyes and an expression that seemed to go from intense concentration to confusion, as if he were always trying to figure something out.

What was she supposed to do? She didn't even know this guy. Still, how could she refuse?

"My mom will like them in the front foyer. We have guests coming tomorrow, and she likes flowers around."

"But these are for you," Christopher said, looking uncomfortable.

Aisha took them, carefully wrapping her hand around the stems. "Thanks," she said. Then, not knowing what else to add, she pushed past him and opened the door. She turned back to him with what she hoped was a dismissive, yet polite expression. "Thank you. I'll see you around."

"Um, wait!" Christopher bounded toward her. "Listen, I, uh, I was thinking."

"Yes?"

He made a fist and slapped it against his palm. "I was, uh, wondering if you'd like to go out with me."

"No, I wouldn't," Aisha said.

Christopher's jaw dropped. "You wouldn't?"

"Thanks, but no."

"Do you already have a boyfriend or something?"

Aisha shook her head. "No."

"Then . . . you just think I'm a troll or something?"

"Look, Christopher, I don't think you're a troll. I just don't know you, that's all. We've only spoken once or twice, and then it was just to say hi."

"Well, if you went out with me, you'd get to know me, wouldn't you?"

"If I don't know you and don't know if I'd even like you, why would I want to go out with you?"

Christopher tilted his head and gave her a sidelong look. "Are you a lesbian? Is that it? No offense if it is; that's cool."

"No, that's not it. I date guys. Only guys. I just don't know you. Maybe later, after a while, I'll get to know you."

"Okay, I'm lost here. You tell me. How do I proceed with getting to know you if I can't ask you out?"

"Why are you so sure you want to know me?" Aisha asked.

Christopher shrugged. "Because you're very beautiful."

"Thank you."

"Besides, I mean, you and I are, like, the only people of color on this island."

"Ah ha!" Aisha pointed a triumphant finger at him. "See, I knew that's all it was. You figure since I'm the only young black woman around and you're the only young black man around that we *have* to be together. Like I have no other choice. See, I understand. Everyone on the island is starting to say, Hey, Aisha, are you going out with that Christopher guy yet? *Yet*. Like it

64

has to happen. Well, it doesn't have to happen."

"But, you have to admit—"

Aisha shook her head. "No, I don't have to admit. I'm not just waiting around here for you to come and sweep me off my feet. I go out with white guys as well as black guys, so it's not just like, hey, check out my skin, now you have to go out with me."

Christopher nodded. "You know, I'm starting to see something in what you're saying. I think you're absolutely right. We needed to know each other better, see, because if I had known you better, I'd have known you were a bitch." He reached for the flowers. "I'll take those."

"Take them," Aisha said, relinquishing the bouquet.

Just then Aisha's mother opened the door and stepped outside. "Is there some reason I hear shouting out here?"

"I'm very sorry, ma'am," Christopher said smoothly. "My name is Christopher Shupe. These are for you." He handed the flowers to Aisha's mother.

Her mother took the flowers and smiled. "They're lovely. I like to have flowers in the house when we have guests. Thank you. I keep wanting to grow a garden, but I never seem to have the time. Maybe next spring."

"Actually, ma'am, there are things you should

be doing now if you want a garden for next season. You need to be putting in bulbs, you know, for daffodils, tulips—"

"Tulips?" Mrs. Gray said, her eyes lighting up. "I love tulips. But I just don't have the time, and there aren't any landscaping companies that operate on the island."

"There's a guy I know who'd do it on either a per-job basis or by the hour," Christopher said. "Me."

"Mother," Aisha warned.

"Aren't you in school?" her mother asked.

"No, ma'am. I've graduated, and now I'm working to put college money together. I cook nights down at Passmores' and I do repairs around the building for my landlady, but I have several days available."

"Tulips," Mrs. Gray repeated, her eyes wandering over the yard.

"Next spring, just like clockwork," Christopher promised.

"You have a deal, young man," Mrs. Gray said. She turned to go back inside. "And thanks for these flowers."

Aisha shot Christopher a poisonous look. He grinned back.

"Fate," he said.

"I don't believe in fate," Aisha said, closing the door in his face.

LUCAS CABRAL

At the Youth Authority
we slept in barracks, a
dozen bunkbeds to a room,
twenty-four guys in all. The
guy in the bunk above me had
tried to poison his father
with Drano. The guy in the
next bed over had sold LSD
to some eight-year-olds. So,
you see, even though by Chatham
Island standards I was a
bad guy, my fellow cellmates
weren't real impressed.

I spent the first year
being bitter. At my dad for
being such a hard case. At
Claire for never once writing
or visiting. I figured that
was the least she could have
done. At life in general.

But after a while, if you're any kind of a human being, you get past bitterness.

I started reading a lot. Used to help some of the other guys keep up with the lame attempts the YA made to deal with our educations. I grew up a little.

One day I was looking through the Weymouth Times and happened on a picture. Zoey. Zoey Passmore, it said right under the photo of her smiling nervously and standing down by the ferry, the place where she had been the only one of all my supposed friends to say a kind word.

Not that I'm bitter.

The article with the picture said she was one of three Weymouth High kids who had been selected to contribute articles to the paper's youth page. I read the two she did when they came out. An interview with the new vice principal and a funny review of the cafeteria's food. Echoes of a place I used to know.

I cut out the picture and pinned it on the wall beside my cot. After a while it grew yellow and frayed, but I kept it. I don't really know why, except that I've learned you have to cling to hope no matter how unreasonable, no matter how or when it appears.

Even if it's just a faded picture of a beautiful girl you barely knew.

Five

"He was groping you," Nina said. She pulled the trigger of her pump water gun and let fly a stream of water that caught Zoey in the neck. Aiming the stream higher, she arced it straight into Zoey's open mouth. "Last time we went to Big Bite, Jake was groping you, and I'm just saying if we go this evening, expect gropage. It's the fresh air or something. It brings out his grope reflex."

Zoey lay back on the webbed chaise lounge, swallowed the water, and held up her hand for Nina to cease firing. She pumped her own green-and-orange plastic water rifle and aimed toward Nina, who lay ten feet away on a matching chair. Zoey squeezed the trigger and nailed her friend's belly button.

"Sorry," Zoey said, raising her aim.

"It's okay, it feels good," Nina said. "It figures. A beautiful, perfectly sunny day like this, and the beaches are crawling with tourists. They could at least wait till tomorrow."

"I seem to remember you whining about the

tourists all being gone. Anyway, soon we'll have the island back to ourselves," Zoey said. She fired, and this time Nina caught the stream in her mouth. "In the meantime, we have my backyard."

Nina adjusted her rainbow sunglasses and the straps of her two-piece bathing suit. "This tan has to last us like nine months."

"Dragonfly!" Zoey yelled.

Both girls trained their water guns on the big insect buzzing by overhead. It flew off up the hill, and Zoey settled back on her chair.

"Jake was definitely groping you," Nina said. "I saw movement under your shirt."

"Okay, so he tried a minor grope."

"He used to be such a nice boy," Nina said regretfully. "Well raised, respectful of his elders, the kind who always says grace before he eats. Now he's become a swine."

"Guys will do that," Zoey said tolerantly. "They're gropers by nature. Just as girls are counter-gropers."

"I wouldn't know, would I?" Nina said. She sighed dramatically. "Maybe this year I should get me one of them. One of them thar' boyfriends."

"Plenty of guys ask you out," Zoey said.

"Nerds. Dweebs. Geckos."

"How about George in tenth grade?"

"He was such a gross kisser. Total tongue,

like he was trying to lick my liver."

"Thanks for telling me that," Zoey said. "That is the grossest thing I've ever heard."

"No, it isn't. I've told you plenty of grosser things than that."

"Time to turn," Zoey announced. "One, two, three!"

Both girls spun on their lounge chairs, turning at the same time so that they were face to face.

"Hit me," Nina said, opening her mouth wide.

Zoey pumped, aimed, and fired perfectly.

"Not all guys are George," Zoey said.

"You're right," Nina said snidely. "Some are Jake."

"He's a good kisser," Zoey said thoughtfully. "I mean, I think he is. It's not like I have a lot to compare him to."

"Tad Crowley," Nina said.

"Better than Tad," Zoey said definitely. She had kissed Tad at a party when she was mad at Jake. He was the only other guy she had ever kissed. Unless you counted Lucas, and that . . . well, that had been different. She'd never told Nina about that. "You should go out with Mike Monahan. He likes you."

"He told you he likes me?" Nina asked.

"Not in so many words."

"Uh-huh. Well, in so many words I have to go use your bathroom." Nina got up from the chair.

She had a webbing pattern across her stomach.

Zoey put down her head and closed her eyes. Nina wasn't back within the expected two minutes, which meant she was either raiding the refrigerator or she'd found something to do for Benjamin. She was letting Benjamin absolutely use her like a servant lately.

Zoey sensed something change, as if the sun had gone behind a cloud. She rolled onto one side and shielded her eyes, staring up at the sky. She saw the outline of a head, with brilliant rays of sunlight blazing behind it.

"Sorry," a voice called down from above. "Didn't mean to block your sun."

Zoey's breath caught in her chest and she sat up quickly, tilting her head to see the face that went with the voice. She knew who it was.

Lucas was gazing down at her from his deck.

"Lucas?" Zoey said in an overbright voice. "Is that you?"

"I wasn't sure you'd remember," he said.

"Of course I remember," Zoey said, still sounding shrill and phony.

Lucas walked to the end of the deck and climbed over the railing. He dropped to the little path that went below his deck and wound down to Zoey's backyard. In an instant he was standing right in front of her.

He had grown in the two years he'd been

away. There was more muscle on him now, though he was still less beefy than Jake. His blond hair was long and kept falling forward into his face.

"Hi," Zoey said.

"Long time, Zoey," he said. He looked her up and down, not coyly but openly. "You look good. I always remembered you as being skinny."

Zoey gulped. Why did her modest pink bikini suddenly feel so incredibly revealing? For some reason she felt a compelling need to straighten her hair. At the same time, a confused feeling of guilt welled up inside her. This was Lucas. She wasn't supposed to be talking to Lucas.

"I heard you were back," Zoey said.

"Oh? Who did you hear that from? Not my parents. They don't officially admit I am back." He smiled wryly. "They don't officially admit I exist."

Zoey could only nod. What was she supposed to say? She glanced nervously toward the house. Nina could come back out at any moment.

"Ahh," he said. "I see. You're supposed to be blowing me off, aren't you? Islander solidarity and all that."

"No, no," Zoey stammered, her cheeks burning.

He laughed. "I remember you being skinny. I don't remember you being a liar. Don't forget, I was born on Chatham Island. I know how it goes." He tilted his head and looked at her speculatively. "Jake McRoyan think he can get rid of me with a little cold shoulder treatment?" He laughed again, this time bitterly. "Where I've been the last two years, you hope that guys don't want to talk to you. It will take more than Jake, and more than my father, to scare me off."

He turned and began ascending the path again. Halfway up, he turned back. "Tell me, Zoey." His face was softer now, his voice more tentative. "How's Claire?"

Zoey shrugged.

"Does she know I'm back?"

"Yes."

He thought for a moment, then nodded. "I notice she hasn't come by to welcome me home. She's with Jake on this, huh?"

Zoey bristled inwardly. Lucas made it sound like it was some secret pact between Jake and Claire. It was more than that. "I'm with Jake on this, too," Zoey said in a voice that tripped as she spoke.

"Yeah, well, give Claire a message for me next time you see her, will you, Zoey? Tell her not to worry so much. Tell her I keep my promises. You tell her that." He gave Zoey a last long look before he walked away.

Six

Zoey spent the afternoon down at the restaurant, helping her parents prepare for the Labor Day weekend crush. She moved beer from the storage room out to the bar coolers, unpacked several heavy boxes of new plates and sent them through the dishwasher, helped her father pull down the greasy vents from the hood over the stove, changed the oil in the deep fryer, and cleaned the entire walk-in freezer.

By the time evening rolled around, she was more than ready for escape.

She changed clothes in the restaurant bathroom and went outside into the fresh, warm air of early evening. She could see that Jake already had his father's big boat warming up. Aisha was on the foredeck with Nina. Claire was standing on the bow looking at something Zoey couldn't make out, with Benjamin just behind her.

Zoey crossed Dock Street and walked out onto the floating pier.

"About time, Zo," Jake called out to her from up on the flying bridge.

"All work and no play, et cetera," Claire said.

"Hey, some of us have to work for a living," Zoey said, climbing aboard the big cabin cruiser. "Not all of us have rich daddies."

Claire smiled. "But your dad is cool, as fathers go."

"Yeah," Nina chimed in, "your dad smokes dope and listens to The Who."

"The who?" Aisha asked, looking blank.

"Big rock band of the sixties," Benjamin said.

"No, he doesn't, not anymore," Zoey said. She could feel a flush creeping up her neck.

"Doesn't what?" Claire asked. "Listen to The Who?"

"He doesn't smoke pot anymore. Can we drop this topic and get going?" She told herself she was irritable because she'd been working all afternoon. But a part of her also felt guilty. She hadn't told Nina about talking to Lucas, and that was unusual. She told Nina everything. Almost everything.

"Zoey," Benjamin said, "you're really not responsible for what Mom and Dad do. You don't have to defend them."

"Are we going for a boat ride or are we picking on Zoey?" Aisha asked, coming to Zoey's defense.

"Can't we do both?" Claire asked.

"Somebody cast off the stern line!" Jake yelled down from the bridge.

"Is that front or back?" Nina asked. "I can never remember."

The boat backed out of the slip and Jake turned it around to face toward open water. They rounded the breakwater, and Zoey waved to some little kids roller blading along the concrete expanse.

As soon as they were out of the shelter of the harbor, the water grew choppy, with wavetops blown white by the breeze. Jake held the boat a quarter of a mile offshore. Zoey could see the well-preserved Victorian homes that lined Leeward Drive, most of which had been converted into inns or apartments.

Chatham Island was shaped like a croissant, with a big bite taken out of the middle. The bite was appropriately called Big Bite pond, a shallow, sheltered body that nearly cut the island in half. The north half of the island was inhabited, with North Harbor at the very tip. The part south of Big Bite was a wildlife sanctuary, with dirt roads and a very few scattered, isolated homes.

It took less than ten minutes to travel the distance from the breakwater to the inlet. Jake guided the boat through the narrow inlet, and suddenly they were out of the wind, on water

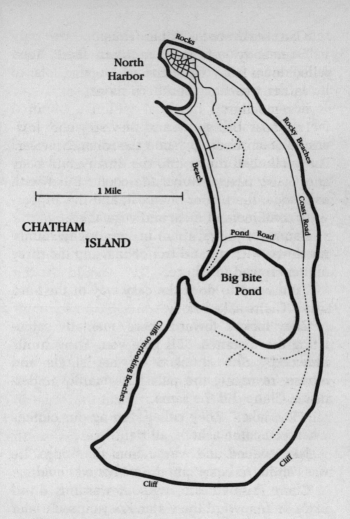

Rocks

North
Harbor

Rocky Beaches

Beach

1 Mile

CHATHAM
ISLAND

Coast Road

Pond Road

Big Bite
Pond

Cliffs overlooking Beaches

Cliff

Cliff

that barely showed a ripple. The pond was only half a mile wide from its northern shore, lined with homes on widely spaced wooded lots, to its wilder, tree-lined southern shore.

Jake anchored the boat within a hundred feet of the south shore and they set about lowering the small dinghy into the water. Nina and Aisha climbed down into the dinghy, and Zoey and Claire passed down the cooler filled with cold soda, the bag of charcoal, and the Tupperware containers of meat and vegetables.

Benjamin joined them in the dinghy, climbing down with a hand from Nina, and the three of them rowed for shore.

"You want to do it the easy way or the hard way?" Claire asked Zoey.

Zoey looked toward shore, mentally calculating the distance. "I'll race you. Loser hunts firewood." She shucked off her shorts and blouse, revealing the pale blue maillot underneath. Claire did the same.

"Hey, Jake!" Zoey called. "Bring our clothes when you come ashore, all right?"

Jake nodded and waved from the bridge. He was waiting to be certain the anchor was holding.

Claire grinned and, without warning, dived like a knife toward the water. Zoey cursed under her breath and dove in after her. The water was cold, but after a day spent in the restaurant kitchen, sweating and covering herself with cleaning solutions, it felt heavenly. She surfaced and saw Claire, already two lengths ahead.

Zoey stretched out her arms and went after her. She was the better swimmer but, as usual, Claire had found a way to get an edge. The distance to shore wouldn't be enough for Zoey to make up for Claire's early start.

Claire stood just as Zoey's feet found the gravel bottom.

"Don't you ever get tired of cheating, Claire?" Zoey asked, squeezing the water from her hair.

"Don't you ever get tired of losing?" Claire replied, grinning.

Aisha rowed the dinghy back out to the boat to retrieve Jake. Claire went back into the water, waist deep, meeting the dinghy just as Jake and Aisha neared shore. She leaned over the side and retrieved her dry clothing. Zoey saw the way Jake's eyes homed in on Claire's cleavage, so ostentatiously displayed in her bright red bathing suit.

If I were the suspicious type, I'd think she did that deliberately, Zoey thought. Jake sent her an innocent smile that proclaimed his guilt. She smiled back with her mouth, letting her eyes tell him that she had indeed noticed.

"Who's coming with me to scrape up firewood?" Zoey asked, looking pleadingly at Nina and Aisha. Both of her friends volunteered halfheartedly. Zoey put dry clothing on over her wet bathing suit and tied her shoes.

"Dry wood this time," Jake said as they tramped into the woods.

"Just tend to your little barbecue, Jake," Aisha said. "I'll be hungry when I get back."

"I don't know if I should leave Jake with Claire, undefended," Zoey grumbled as they shuffled noisily over the carpet of pine needles.

"Which one is undefended?" Nina asked.

"You know, guys are going to look," Aisha said. "They always do, even when they say they don't."

"I don't blame him," Zoey said. "It's Claire, always parading those big buffers of hers around."

"You know Jake's faithful to you," Aisha said, stooping to pick up a fallen tree limb.

"Yeah, he lacks the imagination for anything else," Nina said dryly. "He thinks life comes with a rule book and a set of instructions. He wants to grow up to be exactly like his dad, only with more hair."

Zoey flashed on what her mother had insinuated about Mr. McRoyan at breakfast that morning. She wasn't sure whether she should bring it up or not. Maybe with Nina alone, another time. Somehow telling *two* people seemed like gossip, whereas just telling Nina would be all right. That made two things she was hiding from Nina.

Zoey pointed ahead. "There. Dead tree. We can break off the branches."

"You know what I don't get?" Aisha said. "I don't get Claire and Benjamin."

"No one gets that," Nina said. "Claire's been getting by on her looks since she was twelve. Now she's going out with the one guy who can't be totally sure she isn't a gorgon. Go figure. Not to mention the second part of the equation—what's a nice guy like Benjamin doing with my sister?"

"I don't know about Benjamin being such a nice guy," Aisha said. "No offense, Zoey. I don't mean he's not nice, just that he's . . . he's got an edge to him."

"Of course he does," Nina said before Zoey could answer. "I mean, cut the guy some slack. He's dealing with being blind, which makes you feel weak and vulnerable. So naturally he reacts by keeping his distance from people."

"I think it's all you island people," Aisha said. "You all grew up here together, you're stuck together, so you all get kind of protective of your space."

"We do not," Nina said. "Hey!" she yelled at Aisha. "Don't touch that stick. That's *my* stick. It's much closer to me."

"Very funny," Aisha said with a smile.

"Keep an eye out for ticks," Zoey said.

"Oh, Zoey!" Nina whined. "Did you have to say

the word ticks?" She began examining her bare legs.

"Ticks," Zoey repeated.

"Bats," Nina countered.

"Too early for bats," Zoey said confidently.

"It will be dark soon," Nina said. "That's when the bats come out with their leathery wings and their sharp little teeth."

"Well, at least we haven't seen any snakes yet," Zoey said gleefully, enjoying the crest-fallen look on Aisha's face.

"Yeah, they're worse than bats and ticks put together," Nina agreed solemnly.

"Don't start with me," Aisha warned.

"Psssss!"

Aisha jumped, looking down at the ground where Nina was pointing. Then she shook her head. "Oh, you're very funny, Nina."

"I think we have enough wood," Zoey said.

"Snakes and ticks and bats, oh my!" Nina said.

"Let's just get our wood and follow the yellow brick road back to the beach," Aisha said to Zoey. "See if we can get your boyfriend off her sister."

"It's a dangerous world," Nina said in a low, trembling voice. "Bats and snakes and ticks . . . and Claire!"

The bonfire burned noisily, sending up Fourth of July fireworks in showers of sparks, cooling as they fell to earth before they could reach the dark, overhanging trees.

Clouds had moved in, concealing the stars but letting through the bright diffuse glow of the full moon. Away from the circle of the fire the air had grown brisk, but sitting with her back against Jake's chest, his thick, muscular arms wrapped around her, Zoey was warm. Her toes were close to the fire, and from time to time she had to pull them away to cool off.

Claire and Benjamin were on the opposite side of the fire, visible only in flashes between the flames, sometimes kissing, other times just holding hands. It was odd, always had been, for Zoey to see her brother being romantic. Benjamin, of course, could not see her, or even know that she could see him. It was one of the compensating advantages of being blind, she supposed—you could pretend to have a level of privacy, even when there wasn't any.

Nina and Aisha were down by the water, outlined as shadows against the glittering surface of the pond, having a deep philosophical discussion of some sort as they studiously avoided looking at the two couples.

"Nina needs a boyfriend," Zoey said to Jake.

"Nina needs a personality first," Jake said.

"A guy would be very, very lucky to get her."

"Aisha's the one who needs a boyfriend," Jake said. "I can't believe that new guy Christopher hasn't asked her out yet."

85

"Maybe he isn't attracted to her."

Jake made a dismissive noise. "She's got a nice bod, pretty face."

Zoey twisted around to look at him. "She can read and write, too."

"You know what I meant," Jake said. "The first thing a guy looks at is . . . is looks. Later he gets into whether a girl is smart or has a good sense of humor."

"How much later?"

"Zoey, is it just my imagination, or have you been busting me a lot lately?"

Zoey tilted her head straight back and closed her eyes. Jake kissed her lips and tightened his grip around her, letting his hand slip upward from her waist to just beneath her breasts.

"We've never kissed that way before," Jake observed. "I mean, upside down like that."

"Do I taste like barbecue sauce?"

"We both taste like barbecue sauce," Jake said with a laugh. "Can I have some more?"

"Upside down?"

"Too strange," Jake said. He guided her into turning around. They sat face to face, Zoey's legs over Jake's. She kissed him again, enjoying the feel of his lips on hers.

"That was nice," she said, pausing to breathe.

"Mmmm," Jake agreed.

His eyes reflected the yellow flames, two

separate bonfires burning in dark pools. He undid the top button of her blouse and let his fingers slide beneath the fabric.

"Jake, my brother is like ten feet away," Zoey said in a whisper. Worse yet, Nina wasn't far away, and if she saw Jake in action, she'd be bound to start another round of discussion on groping.

"Your brother is always like ten feet away," Jake said. He let his fingers caress the slope of her breast. "It's not as if he can see what we're doing."

Zoey took his hand and moved it away. She kissed him again, but his response was less than enthusiastic. "Claire isn't blind."

"She's not watching us," Jake said. He reached for her again.

Zoey stood up. "I'm going to talk to Nina and Aisha."

Jake stood up and grabbed her arm. "Just tell me one thing, Zoey," he said. "Is this the way it's going to stay? I mean, I'm supposed to stay on first base until we get married?"

Zoey spun around and faced him. The fire no longer reflected in his eyes. They were just shadows within shadows now. "Excuse me? Did I just hear that?"

"I was just asking whether we're ever going to do it, Zo."

"You said *until we get married*, Jake. I don't remember ever even discussing anything like that."

Zoey put up her hand, palm outward, to keep him at a distance. "We're not even seniors yet."

Jake shrugged. "I didn't mean anything by it."

"Good."

"You know I love you, Zoey," he said softly.

Zoey held her breath. It was not the first time he had said those words. She had even said them to him, once or twice. Maybe she had even meant them, who could be sure? Maybe Jake meant them, too, in his own way. She let Jake draw her close again.

"Don't you ever think about the future, Zo?" he asked in a low voice. "I mean, you know, after high school and all. You ever think about what it would be like to get married and have kids and a house? Maybe a dog."

"Sometimes," Zoey said, feeling uncomfortable.

"I do," Jake said solemnly. "I know we're young, but I think about having a family of my own. Some kids. Maybe a boy."

"Don't you think we should enjoy being wild, irresponsible teenagers?" Zoey asked, hoping to jog Jake out of his serious mood.

Jake smiled crookedly. "I'm not very good at being a wild and irresponsible teenager, am I?"

There was something in his tone that was deeply melancholy. He was right, Zoey knew. Jake was seventeen and already acting like he was thirty.

"You're good at being a horny teenager," Zoey said, leaning her forehead against his.

Jake laughed softly, then grew silent again. "You know what today is?"

"Saturday?" Zoey said.

"Yeah, that too." He nodded his head slowly. Then he turned to look over the placid waters toward the far shore, where house lights shone bright amid the trees. "Wade's birthday."

Zoey felt her heart sink. How could she have forgotten? What perfect timing on her part. This day of all days, she'd stood around chatting with Lucas. She hugged Jake from behind. He took her hands in his and sighed heavily.

"Two years," he said. "I figured I'd be over it after two years. He'd be twenty now, did you know that? Probably a sophomore in college."

"Of course you still miss him," Zoey said.

"Yeah," Jake said. "Someday I'm going to have a son and name him Wade."

Zoey looked away. Benjamin was resting his head in Claire's lap now, sunglasses in place, eyes staring sightlessly up at the gray-black blanket of clouds. Claire stroked his hair in a distracted way and watched Zoey.

No, Zoey realized as Claire's eyes were lit by a spurt of flame from a falling log. It was Jake she was watching.

Aisha Gray

I used to live in Boston, which is a great city, although school there was a drag. I was one of the black kids who got bussed into south Boston so that the previously all white junior high schools there could be integrated. What fun. One day some of the white kids, cheered on by their parents and with the assistance of their older brothers and sisters, decided to turn our bus over. With us still inside.

My folks freaked and decided that was enough of Boston, which was too bad, because really, setting aside that one incident,

Boston was a very cool city. Great shopping.

Naturally my parents, being the people they are, managed to come to the conclusion that the perfect place for us was Chatham Island, a place where people aren't even tan, let alone black. They've never been able to explain their logic. Mostly I think my mom just lost it when she saw this inn for sale and started hallucinating about quilts and valences and canopied beds.

At first I thought people here were even worse than in south Boston. They treated me like I was invisible. They treated my parents and my brother the same way. Always polite, but sort of like we weren't entirely real.

I finally got pissed off and yelled at Zoey. I knew her from school by this point. I said, What is the deal here? You seem too nice and normal to be racist. She was shocked. Racist? I don't care that you're black!

Then what's the damn problem? I said. I'm not invisible.

Of course not, she said. You're just from away.

Away. That's Maine-speak for the entire rest of the planet.

Eventually I stopped being from away. Now I'm not so sure I trust people from away. I mean, I'm polite and all, but still, you don't want to pay too much attention to them for the first year or so.

Seven

Aisha had to run the last several blocks down from Climbing Way, fighting to keep gravity from drawing her too quickly. She made her way down the even steeper drop that was a shortcut over to Dock Street and bypassed Lucas's house, then shifted gears into an all-out sprint along the waterfront as the ferry blew its piercing final warning whistle. She yelled frantically as they raised the gangway, blowing through the gate as she waved her ferry pass in the air. She leapt over the few feet of water that now separated her from the ferry and landed, thankfully, on the slowly moving boat.

Gasping for breath, she bent forward at the waist, hands on her knees, as the eleven-ten ferry pulled away from the dock. Too close. She'd promised her mom she'd go into town, buy potpourri, of all things, at the mall, and pick up the drapes from the dry cleaner. The drapes went in the inn's most expensive room, and the guest who'd reserved the room was arriving on the four twenty-five—which, incidentally, would be the same ferry Aisha returned on unless she managed to get everything done in less than an hour.

Once she caught her breath, she made her way to the bow, squeezing through the cars that jammed the open deck. The car ferry didn't usually make this run, but this time of year the last of the elderly summer residents—the Living Dead, as Nina called them—were starting to bail out, avoiding the Labor Day tourist crush and heading back to their condos in Florida.

She leaned against the railing and looked idly down at the water below, split into two plumes of white by the knife edge of the hull.

"Hi," a voice said behind her.

She turned. Christopher. "Oh, hi," she said coolly.

"Nice run," he said.

"Excuse me," she said, and walked away, squeezing back through the cars toward the stern. She leaned against the rail, watching the wake.

"Hi," he said again.

Aisha sighed. She turned to face him squarely, folding her arms over her chest. "Where are you from?"

He looked surprised. "I was born in Baltimore."

"I see. So you're basically a southerner. That

94

would explain it. See, here in Maine, people have a different attitude toward things than people do in Baltimore. Here, the idea is you leave people alone, they leave you alone, everyone gets left alone." She returned her gaze to the ferry's wake.

"I doubt that you were born here," Christopher said, laughing. "There's no such thing as a black person born in Maine."

"I'm from Boston originally," Aisha said. "But I have embraced the Maine way of life."

"Do you say *ayuh*?"

"Look, no one says ayuh except very old fishermen. And when they do say it, they don't say it like that."

"Do you say *wicked* when you mean something's good?" he asked.

Aisha drummed her fingers on the metal rail. "Sometimes. But that's not what being a Mainer is about. Let me explain again. Whereas someone from Baltimore would go up to a stranger and say hi, a Mainer wouldn't go up to a stranger. Understand, stranger?"

"Ayuh. And it's a wicked good way to be," Christopher said. "Only I'm not a stranger. I'm Christopher Shupe. You're Aisha Gray, a lovely name, by the way."

"I'm also a bitch, or don't you remember that?"

"How could I forget? You're still a bitch."

Aisha narrowed her eyes and glared at him. "Then I would think you'd want to stay away from me."

"Can't. Tomorrow I'm starting in on your mom's garden. That's where I'm headed right now, to the greenhouse for bulbs and fertilizer. Besides, we live on the same small island. Anyway, I kind of like the bitch act. On you it works."

Aisha decided to treat him to silence. Sooner or later he would get tired of annoying her and get the message.

"Your mom seemed nice," he said. "So unlike you. And, no offense, but I think she's got the edge on you in looks, too."

"Excuse me?" Aisha said, breaking her three-second-old vow of silence.

"Maybe it was just that her hair was nicely done, her makeup was very professional, and she has a certain style in the way she dresses." He grinned at her. "But I like you just the way you are—scruffy and bitchy."

"Does this kind of sweet talk work with a lot of girls?"

"I tried to give you flowers."

"I didn't ask you to bring me any damned flowers," Aisha snapped.

"I know. It was sweet of me, don't you think?"

"Sweet," Aisha said poisonously. "Yes, that's just the word I would apply to you."

"Aisha. It means *life*."

She looked at him in surprise.

"I looked it up. You know what Christopher means?"

Aisha coolly looked away.

"You know what Christopher means?" he repeated.

"I don't care what it means."

"It means *boyfriend*."

"No, it does not."

"It will eventually," he said smugly.

"I don't think so."

For once he was quiet, staring off toward the skyline of Weymouth. She began to wonder if she had finally managed to discourage him.

"I have to tell you something," he said.

So much for discouraging him.

"Just look at me, listen to me for one minute. Less, even, if I talk fast, and then I'll leave you alone for the rest of the trip."

Aisha sighed dramatically, and lazily, reluctantly, met his eyes. They were flecked here and there with gold highlights amid the deep brown.

"The day will come, Aisha *Life* Gray, when you and I will stand here on this very boat, wrapped in each other's arms, our lips joined, our eyes closed to everything else around us. Not because you're the only black chick on the island, not because everyone expects us to get together, but because when I first saw you walking down Exchange Street, I froze, I stopped moving, stopped breathing, stopped thinking. In that instant I knew that you were the reason I was on the island, in Maine, on planet Earth."

He moved closer, and Aisha realized she herself was no longer breathing. He raised his fingers to her cheek as if to draw her close. She felt her eyelids grow heavy, her knees grow weak.

Then he stepped back. "No, I'm not going to kiss you now."

Her eyes flew open, suddenly alarmed.

"But soon," Christopher said. He turned his back to her and started to walk away. Then he hesitated. "And when I do kiss you, you'll stay kissed."

Zoey paused outside Benjamin's room. From inside, she could hear Nina reading, her voice barely muffled by the door.

"I sat down on the edge of a deep, soft chair and looked at Mrs. Regan. She was worth a stare. She was trouble. She was stretched out on a modernistic chaise longue with her slippers off, so I stared at her legs in the sheerest silk stockings. They seemed to be arranged to stare at."

Zoey knocked.

"Yeah," Benjamin's voice called out.

Zoey opened the door. Nina was seated in

the rocking chair, eyeing her a little impatiently. Benjamin was lying on the floor, his head on a pillow, legs propped up on the edge of his bed.

"I have the feeling that is not *The Plague* you're reading," Zoey said.

Nina held up a pastel paperback. "*The Big Sleep*. Raymond Chandler. Much cooler than Camus."

"And that's on the suggested reading list for this year?" Zoey asked skeptically.

"No, but it ought to be," Benjamin said. "I was reading it in Braille, but this is easier."

"I volunteered," Nina said, looking a little embarrassed. But then, maybe the color in her face was the result of their sunbathing yesterday.

Zoey decided against bringing up the point that her parents paid Nina to read schoolbooks, not mystery novels. It wasn't exactly her business, and the last thing Benjamin would put up with was his little sister acting like she was his mother.

"Sounds good," Zoey said. "Look, Nina, I'm heading down to the restaurant. They asked me to wait tables for the dinner shift."

"That's okay," Nina said. "I'll stay a little while."

"No," Benjamin said dismissively. "I've been hogging your time enough, Nina, go ahead. I'm being a jerk making you sit here and read to me all afternoon."

"No, you're not," Nina said quickly.

Benjamin yawned. "Truth is, I think maybe

99

I'll catch some Z's. I'm going over to your house later anyway, to see Claire."

Nina closed the book with an audible snap. "Okay, whatever." She smiled frostily at Zoey. "I guess I will walk down with you."

They walked down Camden toward Exchange, threading their way through the crowds of sunburned tourists in their Chatham Island T-shirts and Bermuda shorts. Soon, Zoey knew, these narrow streets, these brick sidewalks, would be empty. You could sled down Camden in the winter when the snow fell.

"I spoke to Lucas," Zoey blurted suddenly.

Nina stopped dead in her tracks and grabbed Zoey's arm, stopping her, too. "You spoke to Lucas?"

"Yesterday," Zoey said, looking away. "When we were out in the yard and you went in to use the bathroom. He came down and said hi."

"He came down and said hi?" Nina repeated.

"Actually, he guessed we were all trying to blow him off. He said it wouldn't work."

Nina fumbled nervously in her purse and produced a cigarette. She popped it in her mouth.

"That is a really strange habit, by the way," Zoey said, starting down the street again.

"Sorry," Nina said. "I started as a goof; now I can't quit. Come on, Zoey, spill."

Zoey took a breath. "He asked if Claire knew

he was back, and he said to tell her not to worry so much. Something about keeping his word."

"Hmm." Nina sucked on the unlit cigarette. "How come you didn't tell me earlier?"

"I was . . . embarrassed," Zoey admitted. "I mean, we're supposed to be doing the big ostracism thing, and right away I blow it."

"What were you supposed to do?" Nina asked. "Turn your back on him?" She grabbed Zoey's arm again. "So. How does he look? Still gorgeous? Or is he all tattooed and mean-looking from being in prison?"

"It wasn't a prison, it was a youth authority. Reform school." Zoey called to mind the image of Lucas, first a silhouette against the sun, then a slightly sullen, somewhat gorgeous guy, standing with arms crossed in her own yard. "Sure he's cute," Zoey admitted. "Not my type, of course."

"No, I wouldn't think so," Nina agreed, giggling as if at some private joke.

"Well, it's not that funny."

"Yeah, it kind of is, Zo. I mean, Lucas is the classic bad boy. Even before he got in trouble over the accident, there had been other stuff. The only thing you ever got in trouble over was that time in seventh grade when Ms. McQueen caught you cheating."

"I was *not* cheating," Zoey said hotly.

"See, that's my point. While you were *not*

cheating, Lucas Cabral was probably shoplifting."

They reached Exchange and Zoey glanced at her watch. She had already, strictly speaking, walked a block out of her way. "I better get on down to work. You could come and hang out if you want."

"I know I have no life, Zoey, but even I can think of better things to do than sit around and watch you work. Besides, now I have to go tell Claire what Lucas said."

"No!" Zoey said. "She'll know I talked to him."

"Relax. I'll tell her *I* talked to him. I'm not afraid of my sister."

"It's not Claire; I don't want Jake finding out. He'll think I'm a traitor or something. You know how he felt about Wade. He idolized him."

"Yeah," Nina answered thoughtfully. "You know, Benjamin said something about that. We were talking about Lucas being back. Benjamin says Jake is overdoing it. He said something . . . It sounded really cool the way he said it. It was something like *the best part of Wade's life was the end of it*. Only it sounded cooler than that."

"Nothing in his life became him like the leaving it," Zoey said. "Shakespeare. I've seen it in my quote books. Kind of a rotten thing for Benjamin to say."

Nina shrugged. "Maybe your big brother knows something you don't."

Zoey

I started working on this idea for a romance novel soon after I first kissed Jake. I guess I figured it would sort of be about Jake and me. I know, it's a dopey idea. What's really embarrassing, though, is that I'm still kind of working on it and I'm almost a senior. Every month or so I'll get this great idea and I'll start writing away at top speed, filling page after page of the big journal I bought just for this purpose.

So far I've written chapter one about twenty times. There is no chapter two.

Sometimes it's a historical romance and I'm the usual lusty yet virginal heroine, a plucky maiden who is captured in a raid on my small village by the hero, who is a lusty, fiery, yet strangely sensitive knight or Viking or prince about to reclaim his throne. The one thing you can be sure of is that he's lusty, fiery, and yet strangely sensitive.

I know it's corny, but that's the way these things are written. I didn't make up the formula. Besides, I do think Jake would look pretty good in armor.

Other times I go with a more contemporary story. Say, one about a lusty yet virginal heroine who, let's say, lives on a small island off

the coast of Maine. This
requires less research.

Unfortunately, I have a
basic problem with this
scenario. You see, one so
seldom encounters a lusty,
fiery, yet strangely sensitive
knight, Viking, or prince
along the coast of Maine.

Eight

Zoey didn't get away from the restaurant till after ten o'clock, her apron stuffed with forty-two dollars in quarters, singles, and the occasional five-dollar bill. Her feet hurt from running and her back from hoisting heavy trays.

The night air was like a slap of cold water on her face. Getting away from the smell of food and beer and people's cigarettes to breathe the fresh, salt air revived her. The thought of heading straight home to sit in her room or watch TV downstairs with Benjamin held no great attraction. Neither did the idea of going over to Nina and Claire's house. The last thing she wanted was to face a cross-examination by Claire.

Instead she stayed on Dock Street as it curved along Town Beach, enjoying an unusually clear sky filled with stars. It was the sort of sky you saw in winter, when the sky got so clear and cold that it seemed like nothing lay between earth and empty space.

She reached the end of Dock, where it

merged into Leeward. She'd expected to head over to Jake's house, just a hundred feet away, a blaze of lights amid the pines. Instead she turned right, following the dark road that led to the breakwater.

There was a sign at the head of the sandy patch that connected the road to the breakwater, stating that no one was to be there after dark. The town had put up the sign after some tourist kids had been swept away by high surf and badly battered before they could be rescued. Naturally, no resident of the island paid the slightest attention. Unlike tourists, residents knew better than to parade around the breakwater when a freak summer storm was sending fifteen-foot waves crashing over it.

To the right, the bay was placid within the shelter of the breakwater. To the left, the sea kept up its relentless attack, churning and surging. Every so often it sent explosions of spray up into the air, carrying on the breeze as a salty dew that condensed on Zoey's warm skin.

It was one of Zoey's favorite places, a walk that never failed to affect her, at once deeply calming and exciting. The slowly flashing green light at the breakwater's tip glowed like a firefly. Across the harbor, she could see light spilling from the restaurant she had just left. Up on the ridge she could pick out the lights from Aisha's inn. And across the four miles of water, Weymouth.

But for Zoey, the better view was always the view north, straight out into a profound darkness unaffected by man-made lights, indifferent even to the stars and the moon.

She neared the end of the breakwater before she saw him sitting on the wall, his legs hanging over the side, seemingly oblivious to the crash of waves at his feet. A fountain of spray erupted, drenching him in a salt shower. He tilted back his head and smoothed his hand over his hair.

Zoey stepped back, hoping to walk away before he noticed her.

"Too late, Zoey," Lucas said. "I've watched you all the way from your folks' restaurant."

"I was just heading over to Jake's house," Zoey said, pointing, as if that would help convince him.

Lucas brought up his legs and stood, shaking his head to throw off a new dousing of water. "I saw you hesitate down at the crossroad. You like it out here? I do. It's one of the places I kept thinking about while I was away. I kept thinking of a night just like this, and the smell of the sea."

Zoey nodded. "It is nice out here."

"You have no idea," he said softly. "You've never had it taken away from you."

"I guess you're right." She paused, gazed back over her shoulder at the lights of Jake's house. "Well, I have to go."

He fixed her with his gaze, curious, confused. Then he smiled a faint half-smile. "Oh. You're scared of me, aren't you?"

"No, I'm not. I mean, you and I used to be friends. You know, neighbors, anyway."

"I used to bring my mom's sweet rolls down and hang out with you and Ben and your mom for breakfast. Your dad would already be down at the restaurant. You'd be telling your mom about school, or what Nina said, or getting upset over the hole in the ozone or whatever." Lucas looked at her and smiled. A real smile this time. "And your mom would be nodding and muttering *uh-huh,* having no idea what you were saying because she hadn't had her first cup of coffee yet. Ben would be sitting there, pretending to read the newspaper upside down." Lucas laughed at the memory. "Does he still pull stuff like that?"

Zoey smiled despite herself. "He's added a few tricks. He walked into a classroom with a substitute teacher last year and acted like he thought he was in the boys' bathroom. He pretended to believe the teacher's desk was a urinal. The sub totally lost it."

"Did he . . . ?"

"No. He's not crude, just strange."

"I always did like Ben. I always liked your whole family. You seemed so nice and normal to me."

"Normal? I don't know about normal. Personally, when I want normal, I go over to—" She fell silent and looked away.

"You can say Jake's name," Lucas said. "That feud is all one-way. I have nothing against Jake McRoyan, except that he hates my guts."

Zoey glanced over her shoulder again, her heart fluttering. For the second time in two days, she found herself talking to her boyfriend's greatest enemy.

"Did you tell Claire what I said?" Lucas asked.

Zoey shook her head. "Not exactly. I told Nina, though." She looked down at his feet. "What did you mean about Claire didn't have to worry, and you kept your promises?"

"Nothing," Lucas said. "Old news, old history. We were kind of close before the accident, Claire and I."

"I know. She's going out with Benjamin now."

"Poor Ben," Lucas said.

"He doesn't think so, I guess. They've been going out for a year almost."

"And you're still with good old Jake, huh?"

"Yes, still." It was so odd, Zoey realized. Here

she was, talking to Lucas as if he were a stranger. Except he was a stranger who knew all the people she knew, knew much of her life, her history. Sometimes when he spoke it was like the old times, an easy, familiar feel, as if he were still the same guy who dropped by for breakfast. Then, suddenly, she would remember what he had done, and why he had been away.

And why Jake, the guy who loved her, and whom she loved in return, so hated him.

"You're looking confused," Lucas said, reading her thoughts. "You don't know how to treat me, do you? Am I the enemy? Or am I still a friend?"

"I guess I don't know," Zoey confessed.

"I know how I feel about it," Lucas said. He turned to look off toward the town. Lights were being extinguished as North Harbor began to go to sleep. "When you're locked up, you spend a lot of time with your memories. At first you tend to focus on all the bad stuff, like how it was you came to be locked up. But you can't spend almost two years reliving the bad times. Eventually you start to remember all the good times. All the places you enjoyed. This place, for example. And all the people you cared for." He looked at her again, his smoldering dark eyes wide and glittering with reflected moonlight. "I remembered Claire, yes. And Nina and Ben and

Aisha. I remembered Wade, too. I even remembered all the times I was out with my dad, working, hauling up the lobster pots, him cursing at me in Portuguese. Even though they weren't all happy memories, they were a million miles away from my cellmates and our cinder-block walls." A dark shadow crossed his face, like clouds momentarily blotting out the moon. Then he looked up at her again, his expression peaceful.

"I also thought about you, Zoey. Strange, because I don't think I'd ever paid much attention to you when we saw each other every day. I don't know that I'd ever really seen you until that day when you . . . when you gave me that ice-cream cone. Still, I found my thoughts returning to you. I think in some way you came to represent everything that I had lost."

Zoey's throat had gone dry. She swallowed hard. A jet of spray shot up, landing as noisy rain in the space between them.

"Now you're really worried, aren't you?" Lucas said.

Zoey shook her head, not trusting her voice.

"It's okay, I understand," Lucas said. "Don't take me too seriously. I've just been around guys who don't talk much except in four-letter words and threats. And then there's my folks. My dad hasn't spoken a word to me. He's forbidden my mother to speak, too, although once when he wasn't around, she . . ." He stopped as his voice broke. He took several deep breaths. "Sorry. They say it takes a while to readjust to normal life. You'd better get going. This island is so small, somebody's likely to see you."

He was giving her the opportunity to leave. And that's exactly what she should do, Zoey knew. This was Lucas. Lucas Cabral, the person responsible for Wade's death.

More important, Jake, Claire—everyone— was determined to make Lucas a pariah. It was a matter of islander solidarity. And if they knew she was giving any sort of support to Lucas, she herself might be the next one cut out of the group.

"Go on, don't feel bad about it," Lucas said. "I know how it is."

Zoey nodded and turned away. She took a half-dozen steps before she turned back. "Lucas!" she yelled.

"Yeah?"

"Why don't you stop by for breakfast some-time?"

"Why don't you stop by for breakfast?" Zoey muttered into the darkness of her room. Was she nuts? Was she coming unglued? Was she absolutely begging for trouble? She tossed in the bed, flipping from her left side to her right side, scrunching the pillow up under her head.

Not enough that she had talked to him, no, not nearly enough. Jake might have forgiven that. After all, he knew she was no good at being mean to people. But no, she'd had to go that one step further. She'd had to make the leap from *dumb, but we can overlook it* to *what on earth were you thinking?*

Still, Lucas had seemed so sad. Sad and alone and . . . well, face it, kind of gorgeous, if you liked guys with smoldering, melancholy eyes. What was she supposed to do? Add to his sadness? Stomp on his sort of sexy vulnerability? What if he'd gone out to the breakwater thinking about suicide? What if it was like the guy in that movie, *It's a Wonderful Life,* that Christmas movie where the guy was getting ready to kill himself and the angel came along to rescue him at the last minute? What if the angel had said *Screw you, pal, no one wants you around*?

It would have been a very different movie.

And it really had nothing to do with the fact that Lucas had great dark eyes.

Nothing.

She was just being nice.

See, Jake had great eyes, too. And Jake didn't end up going to reform school.

114

Whereas Lucas probably hadn't even seen a girl for two years.

She threw back her covers and twisted her Boston Bruins shirt she was wearing back around. She went to the cramped desk in the dormer window and looked for a while down the street, dark under an overcast sky.

She snapped on the little brass light mounted on the wall and sat down, pulling out her journal. She found the paper clip that marked the end of her last version of the romance novel and checked the draft number. Picking up her pen, she wrote:

Chapter One —Draft #23

She'd been wrong all along, she realized. It shouldn't be a story about the lusty yet virginal maiden who is carried off by the lusty, fiery, yet strangely sensitive knight, Viking, or prince. It should be a story about the same knight, only he was lying wounded, nearly dead after a terrible battle. He'd been wandering lost, perhaps not even knowing who he truly was anymore. Wandering lost, bloody, thirsty, hungry, and alone.

He would wander into the maiden's village, where she lived with her ancient, gnarled uncle after her entire family had been killed by marauding barbarians.

The very barbarians who had wounded the knight. That way there would be a connection between the two.

The maiden would take him into her humble, historically accurate yet clean house and lay him tenderly on her straw mattress. She would remove his armor, piece by piece, and hide it in the woods, so if the barbarians came looking for the knight they wouldn't know it was him.

What would he have on under the armor?

A leather jerkin. Whatever that was. But that would have to be removed, too. And the wound would have to be cleaned and bandaged. And the rest of him would have to be cleaned as well. After all, dried blood and so on.

Then she'd spoon-feed him some soup. He'd thank her and ask her name, which would be . . . Meghan. Or Raven. Or Chastity.

Chastity for now, anyway. Later, when the knight recovered . . .

Zoey put down her pen and sat back in her chair. She had covered three and a half pages with her looping, disorganized handwriting, but now a wave of sudden sleepiness reminded her that it was, after all, the middle of the night.

She snapped off her light and went back to her bed.

She was letting her imagination run away

with her, something it often did. All that had happened was she'd spent a few minutes talking to Lucas on the breakwater. It didn't mean anything. Besides, he'd said he remembered her as skinny.

He'd also said she represented everything he'd lost. What did he mean by that?

And why did she care?

Zoey fell asleep with that question running slower and slower around in her mind. And the memory of Lucas's eyes.

Nine

"If you have a touch-tone phone, please press one now."

Aisha pushed the one.

"Hi, this is Christopher. If you'd like the accounting department, please press two. If you'd like the lingerie department, press three. If you'd like to be connected to the space shuttle, press four."

Aisha pressed four.

"Hi, this is Christopher. If you'd like to join a suicidal cult, press pound and five. If you'd like to speak to one of our sales representatives, press star-nine."

Aisha pressed seven, two, and four.

"Hi, this is Christopher. If you'd like to order pizza, press ninety-nine. If you'd like to eat fish, press *E: none of the above*."

Aisha wrapped the cord around her finger and yanked it from the wall.

"Hi, this is Christopher. If you'd like to know what *zeitgeist* means, press the *zeitgeist* button.

If you can spell *waba waba waba waba,* please press *press.*"

Aisha threw the phone at the door.

The door opened. Christopher stood there, grinning his cocky grin. "Hi, this is Christopher," he said.

Aisha woke up in a cold sweat, eyes wide, breathing heavy, and heart pounding. Sunlight blazed around the edges of her curtains. Outside she could hear a familiar *peet-weet, peet-weet* from the sandpiper who had been coming by in the mornings before heading down to the water.

Aisha liked birds. Although she would be relieved when this particular sandpiper decided it was time to head south for the winter. He'd been waking her up lately.

At least he'd put an end to that dream. That *nightmare.*

She put her feet down on the braided rug and rubbed her eyes. The clock said six ten. Thanks to her sandpiper friend, she was already back on a school-year schedule.

Aisha got up, put on her blue terry-cloth robe, and forced a comb through her hair. Because her room was downstairs, just off the common area used by guests at the inn, it was important for her to look somewhat civilized when she came out of her room in the morning. She had to walk through the foyer to reach the little downstairs powder room, where she quickly splashed cold water on her face, taking care to wipe the sink down afterward with paper towels. Everything the guests saw had to be perfect at all times.

The shower in the family bathroom was upstairs in the semidetached wing that included her parents' bedroom, the family room, the small family kitchen, and her mother's office. Her brother Kalif's room was just around the corner in the main house, right beside one of the guest rooms—which meant he was doomed to have a stero- and TV-free room, lest he annoy a guest.

Aisha could hear her mother in the formal downstairs kitchen, preparing coffee and the usual amazing spread of fresh-baked muffins, poached eggs, bacon, and fresh-squeezed orange juice for the guests, at least one of whom already seemed to be waiting in the breakfast room at the rear of the house.

"Aisha," her mother called out from the kitchen in her cheery, fake, for-the-guests voice, "would you be a dear and get the paper for Mr. and Ms. O'Shay?"

Aisha rolled her eyes. Days like this she really wondered about the whole idea of running an inn. Sure, her father's job as a librarian in Weymouth wouldn't let them live like millionaires, but at least wherever they lived it would be all theirs.

Fortunately, winter wasn't far away, and then it would be many weeks between guests. They would slowly take back the huge house, and she'd be able to do wild and crazy things like step out of her room without having her hair combed and a cheerful smile plastered on her face.

Tough, looking quaint and cheerful when you'd just woken up from a nightmare.

Aisha opened the heavy front door and walked out onto the steps. The papers were halfway across the lawn, and she grimaced in annoyance. She was bending over to pick up the *Portland Press Herald* and the *Weymouth Times* when she heard him. The voice straight out of her dreams.

"Hi," Christopher said.

Aisha spun around like a cat, feeling the little hairs on the back of her neck stand up.

"Sorry, I didn't mean to scare you," he said. He was wearing overalls with no shirt on underneath. There was a dirty trowel in his hand.

"What the hell are you doing here at six in the morning?" Aisha demanded, pressing her hand over her beating heart.

121

"I'm starting on the garden," he said.

"The sun is barely up," Aisha said, outraged.

He shrugged. "I have to start early. Mr. Passmore wants me to come in and cook the lunch shift today. Besides," he said with his all-too-familiar grin, "I've been up a long time. They bring the newspapers over on the water taxi at one a.m. the night before and drop them at the dock. I have to pick them up and have them bundled and ready to go before five so the fishermen can have theirs to take out with them for the day."

"Wait a minute, you also deliver the papers? Since when?"

"I just started two weeks ago."

"Exactly how many jobs do you have?"

"Just what I told you: I cook part time at Passmores', I deliver the morning papers, I do a little work around my apartment building, and now I'm starting to do yard work. Also, sometimes I do shopping on the mainland for some of the older folks."

"Are you involved in working with telephones at all?" Aisha asked sourly.

"No. Why?"

Aisha waved off his question. "Never mind. Are you going to school?"

"That's what I'm working for," Christopher said. "I'm accepted for U Mass next year. I have some scholarship money, but I need to save some up, too."

Aisha nodded and started to walk back to the house. On the steps she looked back over her shoulder. "Business major, right?"

"How'd you guess?"

Zoey woke up late and hungry. The day before she had worked straight through what should have been dinnertime. After that she'd had the chance encounter with Lucas at the breakwater and since then, she hadn't really thought about food at all.

She trudged toward the shower, scratching her head and trying to pry open her left eye. She brushed her teeth and started running the water in the shower. It always took a good minute for the hot water to come.

This time, however, it didn't come at all.

"Oh, man," she groaned through a foam of Crest. The hot-water heater must have gone out again, a regular occurrence. Either that, or Benjamin had taken one of his half-hour showers.

She rinsed and stomped barefoot down the stairs, feeling grumpy and sleepy and a little dopey. "Four more and I'd have the seven dwarfs," she muttered.

"The damned hot water is out again!" she yelled as she reached the kitchen.

"I'm sorry to hear that," a voice said calmly.

Zoey jumped, and spun around. She clapped her hand over her heart.

It was Lucas.

Her brother was nowhere to be seen. Neither was her mother. Only Lucas, who was sitting in the breakfast nook and sipping a cup of coffee. A plate of sweet rolls was on the table, two left.

"Your mom invited me to wait for you," Lucas said. "She had to go to the restaurant, then catch the eleven-ten ferry. Ben went with her. Something about school clothes."

"Oh, Lord," Zoey muttered under her breath. She reached for her tangled mess of hair and tried to shove and pat it into something human-looking. But then she realized that with her hands over her head, her Bruins T-shirt rode perilously up toward her cotton panties. She slapped her arms down to her sides and tugged the shirt hem downward, which had the effect of drawing the fabric taut over her breasts. She released the hem and started on her hair again, then crossed her arms over her chest and tried her best to look nonchalant.

"You did invite me for breakfast," Lucas pointed out.

Zoey nodded. "Yes. Yes, of course, because I hoped you'd bring some of those delicious sweet rolls and I see you did so I guess I was right in inviting you . . . not that that was the only reason, I mean it's not like you're the baker or something I mean I . . . we, I mean my mom and Benjamin . . . I also, you know . . . you know, we're like friends and all from before."

Nicely expressed, Zoey, she thought.

Lucas smiled his serious smile. "I guess I kind of surprised you."

"Why? Do I look terrible?" She cringed and took another stab at untangling the bird's nest on her head.

"No, you look wonderful."

"I don't think so," Zoey said, laughing wryly. "I mean, usually I try to wear something more than a T-shirt."

"Trust me, you look wonderful."

"Not that I'm wearing *just* a T-shirt," Zoey added quickly. "I mean, I'm wearing underwear." Instantly she felt the blush rising in her cheeks. She gulped and looked down at the table.

"Me too," Lucas said, grinning at her discomfort.

Zoey sighed. "I'm not exactly awake. When I'm awake, I babble a little less. I still babble, but less."

"Want some coffee? There's still some in the pot your mom made."

"Normally, no, but since the hot water's out

and I'm making a fool of myself, maybe I could use a cup. Or six."

Lucas got up, went to the kitchen counter, and poured. She sat down at the table and reached for a sweet roll. With the first few sips of coffee, her confidence began to return. So she'd babbled, big deal. After all, it wasn't like Lucas had a lot of other alternative conversational partners on the island.

This thought brought guilt with it. Her stomach churned. A mental picture of Jake formed in the air just over Lucas's head.

"Your mom can still cook," Zoey said.

"Yeah," Lucas agreed affectionately.

"Is she . . . are you two talking?"

Lucas shrugged. "My mom is trying to play it safe. She wants to make peace, but if she defies my father outright, well . . . You know my father. He's very 'old country.' He thinks he's the absolute ruler of the house, period, just like he is on the boat."

"Still, he's letting you live there," Zoey remarked, taking a bite of the roll.

"It's all a part of the same thing," Lucas said. "He's Portuguese, *Acoreano*. He's an islander going back in his family to long before Chatham Island had even been discovered by whites. Family is very important, and you have to take care of family no matter what, so no, he won't just kick me out. Not until he can figure out something to do with me, anyway." He rolled his eyes. "Like I said. Very old world."

"But isn't your mom from the Azores, too?"

"No. She emigrated from the Netherlands. The Dutch are a bit looser, I guess." He used his fingers to rake a strand of hair that had fallen over his eye. "That's where I got my blond hair," he said. "Just think Little Dutch Boy."

Zoey patted her own hair with her free hand. "Just think sparrow's nest."

Lucas was about to say something else, but he bit his lip and fell silent. The silence stretched awkwardly for a moment.

"Are you going to be going to school?" Zoey asked.

"Yeah. I still need a year, what with the Youth Authority being so much better at locking people up than it is at education. So, yeah, I'll be going to Weymouth High. I know everyone on the island will be thrilled to find that out."

Zoey nodded glumly and chewed the last bite of her roll thoughtfully. "I guess it will be kind of rough for you."

"And for anyone who befriends me," Lucas said, his voice dropping. "Which is why I want to say something. You've been very sweet, Zoey, but I don't expect you to talk to me in public. I understand how it is. I promise it won't hurt my feelings if you blow me off."

Zoey hesitated. What was she going to do about this? It seemed awfully hypocritical to talk to Lucas here, even to enjoy talking to him, and then pretend that she couldn't stand him later.

Lucas grinned crookedly. It was meant to look tough and indifferent, but the corner of his mouth collapsed a little. "I'm a big boy," he said. "I can handle it."

"No one can handle it," Zoey said. "You can't live life totally cut off."

Suddenly she stopped. She had reached for him without thinking. Her hand, dripping with sugar glaze from the roll, was covering his. Slowly, Lucas's fingers entwined around hers. Neither of them was breathing. Zoey's heart was beating so loudly she was sure he could hear it.

"I . . . I got you all sticky," Zoey said, her voice a squeaky gasp.

Lucas raised their locked hands to his lips. He brought her sugary index finger to his mouth. His eyes were nearly closed, his every movement in slow motion.

The doorbell rang. Zoey snatched her hand away. He withdrew his as well.

"The door," Zoey said breathlessly. "Probably Nina."

"I'll leave through the back," Lucas said.

"You don't have to—"

"Yes," he said regretfully, "I do." He turned away as the doorbell rang a second time. At the back door he paused, looking down at the knob. "Thanks," he said. And then he was gone.

Ten

The front doorbell rang a third time before Zoey reached it. She hoped Lucas was smart enough not to let Nina see him as he climbed back up the hill. "I'm coming, Nina," she muttered. "Jeez, hang on a minute."

She paused for a moment, closed her eyes, and tried to catch her breath. Nina knew her too well. She might easily notice the furious blush on her neck.

Zoey opened the door. Her breath caught in her chest. Claire stood there, looking grim. A few steps behind her, looking uncomfortable, was Jake.

"Claire?" Zoey asked. And then, in a more suspicious tone, "Jake?"

"Morning, Zoey," Claire said coolly. "Do you mind if we come in?"

We? As in Claire-and-Jake *we*? Zoey held open the door. Claire glided past. Jake came up and leaned forward to plant a light kiss on her cheek. She sent him a questioning look, but he just shrugged and made a point of pressing on, like he was in a hurry to get past her.

Claire led the way to the family room, as if she were in her own home escorting guests. She seemed to be barely suppressing some urgent need, but intent on acting in control. She sat on an easy chair, legs crossed like a man, arms wide. A forced smile on her lips was betrayed by a cold, dangerous light in her eyes.

Jake flopped on the couch, alternately scowling and averting his eyes. He shifted every few seconds, uncomfortable with himself, yet clearly sullen and angry as well.

Zoey stood with her arms crossed, looking from one to the other. There was no point in pretending that this little visit was normal.

"What's up?" Zoey demanded.

Claire affected a casual shrug. "We just wanted to talk to you."

Again with the *we*.

"You. And Jake. At nine forty-five in the morning."

Claire made a show of noticing Zoey's nightshirt. "I hope we didn't wake you up."

"No, I was up," Zoey said.

"Won't you sit down?" Claire asked, motioning toward the couch.

Jake patted the cushion beside him.

"Excuse me, both of you, but this is *my*

house," Zoey said. "I'll decide whether I want to sit down or not. Now, I haven't had a shower yet, and I'm not up for a long discussion about the weather, so why don't you two tell me what's on your minds?"

Claire met her gaze and held it, her black-on-black eyes boring into Zoey's. Zoey looked away, then looked back.

"I think you know what this is about," Claire said. "My little sister isn't a very good liar, you know. She said *she* spoke to Lucas, but Nina is weak on making up convincing details."

Zoey tried not to flinch or show any guilty reaction, but the result was that she just stood there in the middle of the room, staring stonily.

"Look, Zo," Jake said, "it's no big deal if, you know, he kind of took you by surprise and you talked to him for a couple of seconds or whatever. I mean, like I told Claire, you're a nice person. Your natural instinct is to be nice."

"How nice of you to defend me to Claire," Zoey said sarcastically. "When did this little discussion take place?"

Jake wrinkled his brow and looked upset, but Claire stepped in smoothly. "I called him last night. Also, we discussed it on the way over here."

"On the way over? You live on the point, Claire, and Jake is down island from here."

"I asked him to pick me up in his truck," Claire said blandly.

"This is amazing," Zoey said. "What is this, the Spanish Inquisition?"

"We're just asking, Zo, did you talk to Lucas?" Jake smiled placatingly. "That's all. Simple question."

"What if I don't want to answer your simple question?" Zoey said, trying to buy time. What could she say? They were just asking about her very brief conversation with Lucas in the backyard. They didn't even know about the breakwater, or that he'd been there just minutes before, raising her fingers to his lips—

"You're no better at lying than Nina is," Claire said contemptuously.

"Are you calling me a liar?" Zoey asked, loading her voice with outrage.

"I'm saying you talked to Lucas Cabral," Claire said, unintimidated. "It's a yes or no answer."

Zoey glanced desperately toward Jake, but his gaze had hardened, drawing on Claire's determination.

"I spoke to him."

"Damn it!" Jake exploded. He shot to his feet and began pacing angrily back and forth.

Claire nodded. "So. What did he have to say?"

"Who cares what that creep had to say?" Jake stormed. "I thought you understood, Zoey. I mean, what were you thinking of? Did you at least tell him to hump off?"

"He caught me by surprise," Zoey protested weakly. "I was out back sunbathing and suddenly he's talking to me. I didn't know what to do." She flopped her arms at her side.

"Tell him the truth," Claire suggested. "I'm sure he won't be surprised. Just tell him we don't talk to people who do the kinds of things he did."

"I don't think he did it on purpose," Zoey said. Instantly she realized she'd made a mistake.

Jake whirled on her, his face contorted in rage. "On purpose? Who the hell cares if it was on purpose? He was drunk and he got behind the wheel of a car. Maybe he didn't say, 'I'm going to ram this car into a tree and kill Wade McRoyan,' but he knew he was drunk and he knew he was driving, end of damn story. If I go running around town shooting off a gun, maybe I don't *plan* to kill anyone, but if I do, I can't just shrug my shoulders and say, 'Hey, sorry, pal, I didn't plan to kill you.' It doesn't matter. You're just as dead."

Zoey recoiled, startled by Jake's rage. But at the same time his words hit home. He was right, wasn't he? Lucas might seem like a perfectly nice person, even a sad, lonely person in need of a friend, but did that change what he had done?

Wade was dead. That was reality. The guilty thrill she'd felt when Lucas told her she looked wonderful, the disturbing warmth that had flowed through her when he kissed her hand . . . that was illusion. Reality was Wade. And Claire, not her closest friend, perhaps, but not an enemy, either. And Jake, his fury now softening into a look of confused betrayal.

The line had been drawn very clearly. On one side: Jake. And Claire, and to a lesser extent Nina and Aisha. On the other side Lucas. Just Lucas.

Zoey drew in a deep, shaky breath. "I . . . I'm sorry. I guess . . . I mean, it never affected me directly. I didn't really know Wade that well, him being older and all."

"You know me well," Jake said softly. "I know you didn't mean any harm, Zo. But this is important to me. See, I want that bastard out of my life, and I want it to work out peacefully, no trouble for anyone. And that only works if we all stick together on this."

"I understand," Zoey said numbly.

"If you love me . . ." He smiled crookedly. "If you just even care about me, you'll stay away from Lucas Cabral."

Zoey nodded mutely and bit her lip.

Claire smiled brightly, as if everything were perfect again. She slapped the arms of her chair and rose to her feet. "Well. That's over, at least."

"You want me to drive you back?" Jake asked.

"Not necessary," Claire said magnanimously. "It's nice out."

"You want to do anything today?" Jake asked Zoey, striving for an air of normalcy.

"I still haven't had a shower or breakfast yet," Zoey said, adopting his tone. "How about if I come over to your house later?"

"Sounds good," Jake said gratefully. He kissed her on the lips, a hurried, uncertain kiss.

Claire was at the door to the breakfast nook, looking thoughtfully at the table. In a flash, Zoey realized one of Mrs. Cabral's famous sweet rolls was still on the table.

Claire went on toward the door, Jake following behind. "I realize this is tougher for you, in a way, than for the rest of us," Claire said, eyeing Zoey thoughtfully. "After all, Lucas is your next-door neighbor."

Jake opened the front door and walked out into the morning sun, looking as if he were glad to be escaping some prison. Claire waited till he was halfway across the lawn, then she favored Zoey with her cool smile. "Plus, Lucas always was cute. Those soulful eyes. That slightly lost look of his. Hard for any girl to resist."

She let the faintest sneer form and then disappear, swallowed up in a brightly artificial smile.

She knows, Zoey realized. Not everything, not the details, but she knows he was here this morning.

"He had a message for you," Zoey blurted.

The way Claire's mouth opened in surprise and her face seemed to pale was very rewarding.

"Oh. Did he?"

"He said you shouldn't worry so much. He said he keeps his promises."

Claire's brow furrowed. For a moment her eyes were genuinely troubled, far, far away as if she were listening to some faint, distant music. Then, with an impatient shake of her head, she put her mask of indifference back in place. "How cryptic."

"What does it mean?" Zoey asked.

"I have no idea," Claire said.

Zoey ended up taking a cold shower, which did very little to improve her mood. To make things worse, she forgot to rinse the shampoo out of her hair, which meant she had to get back under the cold spray after she'd already started drying off.

It had been a completely unsettling morning.

She dressed and spent a few minutes looking through her quote books for some insights. The only things that stood out made her feel worse, not better. Good old Confucius saying, *To know what is right and not to do it is the worst cowardice.*

It sounded good, but of course her problem was that she didn't know what was right. She was perfectly balanced between two opposite points of view:

1. Lucas had paid the price for what he'd done and had a right to be forgiven.
2. No, he didn't.

And there were complications making either point of view hard to completely accept.

Complication #1:
Her boyfriend and one of her friends would completely turn against her if she didn't go their way, and others would follow them.

Complication #2:
Whenever she remembered Lucas kissing her fingers, her knees buckled, her throat seized, her eyes closed, and her head tended to loll back and forth as if there weren't any muscles in her neck.

Complication #3:

Complication #1 made her seethe. Jake actually *conspiring* with Claire.

Complication #4:

Complication #2 made her feel like a treacherous, disloyal, lowlife tramp.

Her eye settled on a well-known saying from Thoreau: *If a man does not keep pace with his companions, perhaps it is because he hears a different drummer. Let him step to the music which he hears, however measured or far away.*

Easy for Thoreau to say. He wasn't trapped on a tiny island with people who knew everything you did within twenty-four hours of the time you did it.

Still, she wrote down the quote and stuck it on the wall beside her window. Then, after a moment's hesitation, she added the Confucius quote, too.

Okay, so maybe she was a coward. Or maybe she was just confused.

She had to get out of here, that much was certain. Any minute now Nina would come by and she'd have to go into the whole thing blow by blow, word by word. And if she told Nina about the breakwater, or worse yet, what had happened that morning with Lucas (knees buckling, throat choked, eyes very heavy, head sinking toward her right shoulder) . . . well, she'd inevitably spill it to Claire, who would undoubtedly have to talk it over with Jake.

Zoey pressed her lips into an angry line. The nerve of those two, coming over and trying to discipline her like she was a naughty child.

Definitely had to get out of the house. She glanced at the clock on her dresser. No, off the island! She could just make the eleven ten if she didn't blow-dry her hair.

She had completely forgotten what Lucas had said about her mom and Benjamin taking the eleven ten until she saw them up by the front rail of the *Titanic.* Benjamin was leaning over the rail, his hands clasped. Her mom was sitting in the passenger seat of a van, chatting with the driver, who happened to be the woman who ran the island grocery store. Her mother noticed her and waved a casual hello.

"Hi, Benjamin," Zoey said as she came up beside him.

"Hey, Zoey."

The whistle blew shrilly and the ferry began backing away from the pier.

"You decide to come shopping with us?" Benjamin asked.

"Actually, I didn't know you'd be here," Zoey said.

Benjamin turned to show her a dubious grin. "Lucas didn't tell you?"

"Maybe he did, but I forgot," Zoey said, feeling a little annoyed. She'd escaped a cross-examination by Nina, only to run into one from Benjamin.

"So, you *did* talk to him this morning."

"Kind of."

The ferry began to pull clear of the dock and headed across the harbor, blasting its horn at a careless sailboat that was getting too close.

Benjamin removed his shades and rubbed his eyes with his free hand. "Damn pollen is thick today. It doesn't seem fair if your eyes aren't going to work that they should itch."

He turned toward her, his dark eyes blank, their focus aimed just slightly to the left of her. Then he pulled a tiny bottle of Murine from the pocket of his jeans, tilted back his head, and settled two drops in each eye.

Zoey felt relieved when he replaced his shades.

"A little eerie?" he suggested.

"What?"

"My eyes. They look weird, don't they? I mean, I can imagine. Like the lights are on but no one's home inside?"

"Benjamin—" Zoey stopped herself from saying something kind. Benjamin was always laying out these little traps, looking for some sign of pity that he would pounce on unmercifully. "Actually, you just looked like you were very interested in my left ear."

"Roger." He gave a little salute. "Adjust three points to starboard. Nice day, huh? Partly cloudy?"

"Yeah. Although the sun is getting lower on the horizon every day."

"It will do that. So, aren't you worried Jake will have a hissy fit if he finds out you're talking to Lucas? You're crazy if you think he won't hear about it."

"He already has. He and Claire came over this morning. Nina told Claire—you remember her, your girlfriend?—Well, Nina told her I spoke to Lucas the other day. We exchanged about a dozen words at the time, so naturally it called for a major inquisition." She related the events of that morning to her brother, leaving out all mention of certain things Lucas had said and done.

"Claire, huh?" He nodded thoughtfully.

"Don't worry," Zoey said. "I don't think it's like she's interested in Jake or anything. I think it's just that they both are all hot about this whole Lucas thing."

"If Claire decides it's to her advantage, she'll find a way to get interested in Jake real fast,"

Benjamin said. "You know how she is. Or maybe you don't."

"You make it sound like she's the one behind all this," Zoey said impatiently. "It was Jake's brother who died. He's the one who's most involved. He's the one I'm worried about hurting."

"Then why is Claire getting in the middle of it all?"

"She was hurt in the accident. I guess she figures she could have been killed, too."

"But she wasn't."

"No."

"So why the big push from Claire?"

She looked at him quizzically. He must have felt her gaze because he smiled at her. "Are you trying to tell me something?" she asked.

He pursed his lips. "I can't tell you anything, little sister. Only . . . you remember that first time we went whale watching? Maybe not, you were pretty young. But it's one of those memories I hold on to from when I could see." He made a wry face. "Like I remember your face, except you'll always look about ten years old. Anyway, I remember the way you could watch the surface of the water, the way it would seem to bulge, almost imperceptibly, and you'd know the whale was right there, just below the surface. You couldn't see him yet, but you knew he was coming up."

"I do remember that. Like a bubble."

He nodded. "That's what we have here. Something big, just below the surface. You can hear it in Claire's voice since Lucas came back. You can feel its outlines in strange things like the two of them coming to see you this morning. And then there are all the little things that don't quite fit in."

Zoey looked at him sharply. "What little things?"

"I'll give you one." He held up his index finger. "The car they were all in that night was an old VW bug, right? Two seats in front and no way a third person fits in."

"Okay."

"So one person's in the backseat. Wade. Lucas. Claire."

"Either Claire or Wade," Zoey said, but the little hairs on the back of her neck were standing up

"Yep. Only . . . only you'd figure the two in the front would be the two who were most badly injured in a head-on crash into a tree." He shrugged. "Wouldn't you figure that?"

"Have you ever mentioned that to Claire?" Zoey asked.

He shook his head. Then he grinned. "But you'll mention it to Nina, which is almost as good."

"So . . . So what are you saying?"

Benjamin made a "who knows?" face. "You know me," he said, waving his hand dismissively, "always picking at details."

Claire

My mother died when I was thirteen. She had breast cancer.

Naturally, I was overwhelmed. I couldn't eat, couldn't sleep without having horribly sad dreams. My dad was great, doing his best to take care of me, sending me to counseling, even asking if I wanted to start going to church.

We'd always been close, my dad and I. Just like Nina had always been closer to my mom. Everyone said they were so alike, not just in looks but in personality. Nina went away to stay with our aunt and uncle for a couple of months, so I didn't see much of

her during this time. And when she
came back, she seemed so changed.
Maybe I was, too.

I know that from then on, things
were different between Nina and me.
Maybe she resented being sent to
stay with my aunt, but I know my
dad did what he thought was right. He
said that as close as Nina was to my
mother, she needed a change of scene.

After the crash that killed Wade
McRoyan, my father never left my
hospital room, even though the doctors
told him it really wasn't a big deal,
just some minor injuries. He asked
me who was driving, and that's when
I realized I didn't remember anymore, which was kind of frightening.

He said he'd get to the bottom of

it. I shouldn't worry. One way or the other he would protect me. He believed in me. He trusted me. He knew I was going to be just fine, because he would never again let anyone or anything hurt me.

It was what I needed to hear right then, with my mind a scrambled mess of half-memories and confusion. At a time like that, you need to hear that it's all going to be okay. You know?

And it was. I healed right up. Lucas confessed. Over time my confusion diminished. Life went on.

Eleven

"It's fine by me," Nina said. "I hate to be responsible for their deaths, anyway. Screaming as they hit the boiling water, crying out to their lobster gods for mercy."

Claire laughed. From time to time, amid the general weirdness, Nina could actually be funny. "Lobster gods?"

"Oh, absolutely," Nina said solemnly. "Lobsters are quite devout. I've never seen a lobster covet or bear false witness."

"What's the holdup?"

They turned and looked at their father. Burke Geiger came up to the seafood counter, pushing a grocery cart that held a bottle of white wine and a loaf of French bread.

"No lobsters," Claire said.

"No lobsters?" her father echoed disbelievingly.

"We're too late," Nina said. "Labor Day's a big day for lobsters, I guess."

"We have to have lobsters," Mr. Geiger said flatly.

"They have no lobsters," both girls said at once.

Mr. Geiger made a face, wrinkling the tan brow that contrasted so sharply with his prematurely white hair. "Let's walk down to the dock and see Roy Cabral."

"If he had any lobsters, he's probably sold them," Nina said, sounding hopeful.

"He'll take care of us," Mr. Geiger said easily, abandoning the basket and leading them toward the door. "Hell, I own half his boat."

Claire hurried to keep up with him. Her father habitually walked as if he were late for a meeting with the president, even when, like now, he was not at work. "Since when do you own part of Mr. Cabral's boat?" Claire asked. She always tried to show an interest in her father's business. He had no one else to talk to.

"And which part?" Nina mumbled, bringing up the rear.

Mr. Geiger shrugged. "You remember a couple of years back, the price of lobster was way down—"

"Sure," Nina said ironically. "You know how I keep up with seafood prices."

Mr. Geiger ignored her. "He was hurting for cash, so I helped out a little. No big deal."

They reached the dock and veered across to the spot where Mr. Cabral's boat was tied up. He was on the boat, hosing down his deck, wearing high rubber boots over dirty overalls. His face had little in common with his son's, Claire reflected, at least as she remembered Lucas's face. Maybe the mouth was the same, but the rest was as hard as chiseled stone, weathered a deep chestnut color.

"Hi, Roy," her father called out.

"Mr. Geiger," Mr. Cabral said, nodding. He turned off the hose and wiped his hands on a rag.

"Roy, I'm in a bind. No lobsters, and my housekeeper is set on cooking up some lobster tonight."

Mr. Cabral nodded again, as if this were indeed a terrible tragedy. "I have lobster. Not all sold yet. Only maybe not so big." He shrugged.

"I'll take whatever size you have, Roy, and thanks."

Mr. Cabral walked back to the hold and began banding and boxing lobsters.

"Smaller are better, anyway," Mr. Geiger said to Claire. "People think you need a lobster the size of a Volkswagen, but the smaller ones are so much more tender."

"Volkswagen," Nina echoed, looking puzzled.

"Yes?" Claire said, batting her eyes condescendingly at her sister.

Nina shrugged. "Nothing. Zoey was talking about Volkswagens today. Wasn't that the car—

you know, the big crash, wasn't that a Volkswagen?"

"I don't know one car from the next," Claire said dismissively. "It was small. Are Volkswagens small?"

Nina shrugged again.

"What was she asking about the car for?" Mr. Geiger said, sounding casual and keeping his gaze fixed on Mr. Cabral.

"I don't know," Nina said. "I was trying to get her to loan me this pair of shorts she just bought. She said she and Ben were talking about it on the ferry this morning. Volkswagens and whether they were small. Ben said he thought it was strange that everyone didn't get crushed."

"That's a little morbid," Claire said disapprovingly.

"He's *your* boyfriend," Nina said. "If you don't like him, maybe you should—"

"Here you have," Mr. Cabral said, lifting a box of sluggishly moving lobsters onto the pier.

"How many?" Mr. Geiger asked.

"Six, half-dozen," Mr. Cabral said. "Two each because so small."

"Could you add a couple more?" Mr. Geiger asked. He turned to Claire. "I thought maybe we'd invite Benjamin over tonight. It's been a while since we've had him to dinner."

*   *   *

Claire leaned against the railing of the widow's walk and watched him approach. He had his cane out, swinging it back and forth in a short arc that was more a formality than a necessity. It wasn't the cane that told him precisely when to stop, stretch out his left hand and place it within three inches of the latch to her gate.

There was always something a little amazing in the way Benjamin managed to find his way through the narrow streets of North Harbor, going the length of Camden, crossing four other streets, taking the right turn on Lighthouse, crossing yet another street, finding her gate among the others on the block, finding the door and the knocker, and ending up there under the porch light, looking as if it were nothing.

He had explained it to her before: seventy-one steps from his house to the first street, and eleven steps to the other curb. Then a hundred eight steps, and ninety-seven steps more. And with all the counting went the sounds: the barking Labrador retriever, the beeping of the video machine just inside the grocery store, the way the sounds of the dock echoed up the cobblestones of Exchange, the lapping surf when you reached Lighthouse.

It was one of the things that made her like him, the way he paid such close attention to all that went on around him. When she spoke to him, he heard her every nuance, focused his full attention on her. Most guys sent every third glance in the direction of her chest and heard only half of what she said.

It also made her uncomfortable at times, the way he always seemed to be paying unnatural attention to details no one else even noticed.

"Hi," she said, panting a little from the hurried descent from her room.

"Yes, I'd like some fudge, please? With walnuts."

"Come on in," Claire said.

"You mean this isn't Mrs. Laskin's sweet shop?"

Claire slipped her hand around the back of his neck, drew him toward her, and kissed him on the lips.

"Why, Mrs. Laskin. I didn't know you cared." He folded the collapsible cane and set it on the small table at the base of the stairs.

Claire's father came out of his study and clapped a hand on Benjamin's shoulder. "Ben, good to see you."

"Evening, Mr. Geiger. How's business? Foreclosed on any widows or orphans lately?"

Mr. Geiger managed a pained but tolerant smile. "Mid-Maine Bank never forecloses on widows or orphans, Ben, you know that. We don't give them loans in the first place."

Benjamin laughed, which delighted Claire's father. Mr. Geiger had made it clear he was somewhat uncertain of Benjamin's prospects, but at the same time he clearly liked him, which was an improvement over Claire's previous boyfriends. In fact, he'd seemed almost eager that Benjamin come for dinner tonight.

"I think Janelle has dinner just about ready, so we can go on into the dining room," Mr. Geiger announced. "Nina!" he shouted up the stairs.

"I'm here, I'm here," Nina said, appearing at the top of the stairs and trotting down them loudly.

"You might try wearing something decent when we're having someone over for dinner," Mr. Geiger said disapprovingly. Nina was wearing bib overalls under an unbuttoned red plaid flannel shirt.

"Really, Nina," Benjamin chided. "Where's your sense of style?"

Dinner was served in the formal dining room, patterned china and lead crystal glittering brightly beneath a brass chandelier. Janelle, the live-in housekeeper Claire's father had hired soon after the death of Mrs. Geiger, served in courses of a cold scallop appetizer, a salad, then the lobsters for everyone except Nina, who had decided in the end that she couldn't cause any more lobster suffering. She had broiled cod instead.

"So, are you looking forward to school starting tomorrow?" Mr. Geiger asked as Janelle poured coffee.

Benjamin shrugged. "It will be my senior year. I guess I'm looking forward to getting it over with."

"And then?"

"You mean after I graduate?"

"It's not a million years in the future, is it?" Mr. Geiger asked.

"He's sizing you up as a marriage prospect," Nina said darkly, stirring sugar into a cup of coffee.

"Me?" Benjamin asked in astonishment. "Marry your father? Well, naturally I'm flattered, but—"

Claire reached across the table and put her hand on Benjamin's. "Don't pay any attention to my annoying sister."

"He never has," Nina muttered.

"I was just curious," Mr. Geiger said. "You're obviously too bright to miss out on college. But at the same time I know your folks have to send both you and Zoey at the same time. Quite an expense."

"Daddy," Claire chided. Her father had a tendency to be rather blunt where money was concerned.

"Oh, Benjamin's a big boy. He knows I hold the loans on Passmores' Restaurant. There's nothing sinister in it. I'm the president of the bank; I'm supposed to know how much money everyone has." He made a deprecating face. "Ben's dad knows what everyone likes to eat, his mom knows how much of what poison everyone on the island drinks, and I know how much money people have."

"Like a dentist knows how many teeth everyone has," Benjamin said. "Or a proctologist knows how big—"

Claire squeezed his hand sharply.

"Thank you, Ben," Mr. Geiger said, shooting Claire a look that was half-amused, half-annoyed. Claire kept her expression innocent. "What I was getting around to was reassuring you that if you need a little boost with the old college funding, I'm sure we at the bank can work something out."

Claire felt the sudden tension in Benjamin's hand. Or perhaps he was just responding to her own surprised reaction. Her father was volunteering to help pay Benjamin's way through college? What was this all about? She stared closely at her father's face, but he was blandly spooning up the ice cream Janelle had put in front of him.

"That's very nice of you," Benjamin said guardedly.

"See?" Mr. Geiger said. "It's not all foreclosing on widows and orphans. Sometimes being a banker you get to help someone out."

Benjamin smiled. Her father smiled. Even Nina smiled, in a sort of perplexed way.

Claire pushed away her dessert. No, this was not what it seemed. Not that her father was incapable of being generous; he was. But Claire knew him too well. They were two of a kind in many ways. Her father had some motive for this sudden display of openhandedness.

As usual, Benjamin went with unerring accuracy right to the point. "So, if I end up taking out a loan, Mr. Geiger, what do I have to sign over to Mid-Maine Bank? This isn't one of those deals where I have to sell my soul, is it?"

"Dad doesn't believe in souls," Nina said.

"Of course I do," Mr. Geiger said. "I'm not just a materialist—I believe in patriotism, honor, right and wrong." He paused to take a sip of his coffee. "And of course, loyalty. Loyalty is especially important to me."

Hopes . . .

Zoey

My hopes for this school year? Well, I'm hoping to get good grades, of course. And I'm also hoping I get a locker combination that's easy to remember. I'm hoping no one talks me into running for student government again because last year when I came in fourth behind Carla Bose, Ted Froman, and Beavis, it was totally humiliating. Although I beat Butthead by two votes.

Claire

Hopes? Hmm. I'd like teachers who understand that homework is an infringement on my private life. I'd like to learn that George Noble had a sex-change operation over the summer so he'd stop asking me out. I'd like people to quit coming up to me and asking what's the deal with my weird little sister, is she nuts or what? That would be nice. Oh, and I'd love to catch the weasel who wrote my phone number in the boys' bathroom and hurt him badly.

Aisha

Desks with some padding. That's

it. And lighter books. I mean, what's the matter with paperbacks? Is there some rule that schoolbooks have to weigh fifty pounds? Also, I hope the lunchroom will figure out that vegetables are not actually supposed to be gray and so overcooked, you can suck them up through a straw. I'm serious. I could show you green beans that would make you cry.

Nina

Hope? Absolutely! I'm brimming with hope. I'm blowing chunks of hope. I hope everyone will like me, and I'll like them, and all my wonderful teachers will fill my head with useful yet interesting information, and all our teams will be in first place and then, yes, I'll be voted queen of the junior prom! Hooray! Failing that, I'm hoping school isn't the usual dark, mind-numbing, spirit-destroying hell it was last year.

Twelve

"And I-I-I will always love you-ou-ou-ou-ou . . ."

"Oh, shut up, Whitney." Zoey slapped the music alarm and threw back her covers. She stood up, feeling pins and needles in the soles of her feet as they hit the floor. She twisted her Boston Bruins shirt around and groaned.

The light coming in through the dormered window was watery and gray. A light that signaled it was too early in the day for people to be up and walking around and scratching themselves. She glanced at the clock. Six twenty-one.

Then she remembered. School.

The day before, Labor Day, had passed in a whirl of work. One of the waitresses at the restaurant had quit, and another had fallen off a bike and bruised her hip. Zoey had been stuck working a double shift, which left hardly any time to think about the fact that in the morning . . . *this* morning . . . she'd be going to school.

At six twenty-one in the morning.

It seemed like a million years since she had gotten up this early to go to school. She had to make the seven-forty ferry. Get to Weymouth at five after eight. Make it up to the school by eight thirty. Catch the four o'clock coming home, arriving four twenty-five.

The times of her life. The rigid schedule of her days. Freedom a thing of the past. Sleep also a thing of the past. Homework.

Still, she realized with a slow, building excitement, she was a senior.

How did a senior dress? Should she do her hair differently? Would she no longer get zits now that she was a senior? Would her hair be easier to manage? Would she acquire great wisdom?

She felt a little clenching in her throat. It would be the same old school, yes, but *she* would be different.

And that could change everything.

"Welcome to the jun-gle, we got fun and ga-ames . . ."

"No, no, please say it isn't so," Nina groaned, pulling her pillow over her head and reaching for the button to silence Axl Rose. "How can summer be over?" she demanded of her pillow. "How?"

She peeked from under the pillow at her clock. "Six twenty-five? Why? Why can't they start school at noon? No, after noon. Then we wouldn't have to eat the food."

She sat up and stared across the room. "Notebooks," she cried, glaring hatefully at the pile of school supplies. "Number-two pencils! Oh, and three-ring binders! It's not right, it's not fair, why me, O Lord, why?"

She kicked at her tangled covers, and continued to kick after they had all fallen off the bed. Then she swung her feet onto the floor and fumbled in her bedside table for her pack of cigarettes. She popped one in her mouth and sucked on it.

School. School. The horror. The loathing. The bad food.

The crush of bodies in the halls between classes. Bells going off. Lockers that jammed. Other girls who all had great hair. Teachers who droned on and on and on till your head started nodding and your eyes grew heavy, heavy, and . . .

Nina snapped herself awake. She had drifted back onto her pillow. No, missing the ferry would not be a smart way to start eleventh grade.

Eleventh grade. A junior. Big deal.

Of course, now with school starting up again, she'd have to spend even more time reading to Benjamin. And maybe Claire would find some new guy. And Lucas was back.

No. No point in trying to work up any enthusiasm. It might be occasionally amusing, but it was still school.

Beethoven's Seventh Symphony, the melancholy, majestic second movement, woke Benjamin from his sleep. He had set up his CD player with this wake-up music, chosen from his eclectic collection of more than two hundred CDs, albums, and tapes, all with his own Braille tags.

He let it play on as he rose from his bed. Right from the front corner of his bed, one, two, three to his bathroom door. The music played in there, too, pumped through two waterproof speakers.

He turned on the shower, waiting till it reached the right temperature, and climbed in. He dropped the soap and had to feel around the bottom of the shower stall for several seconds before he located it, sweeping his hands methodically over the tiles.

He toweled off in front of the sink, facing the mirror that he knew would be steamed and opaque. He wondered, not for the first time, what it would show. Here he was, first day of school, new people to meet, new teachers to deal with, and he had no idea what he looked like.

People told him he was very good-looking, but then, people tended to be kind. Besides, even if he were, what *kind* of good-looking? Good-looking effeminate? Good-looking rugged? Good-looking cute?

"I could be a simp. I could be a toad," he said philosophically. Beethoven swelled toward a stately crescendo, and Benjamin grinned at the darkness where his reflection would be. "Still, at least if I am, I'm a senior toad."

Claire woke through gauzy layers of dream, surfacing, breathing deeply as if she'd been submerged. The alarm was buzzing, and she silenced it and listened for the sounds of the house. The radio on Nina's alarm was playing rock and roll, a faint but unmistakable sound. Her father's shower was running. Outside, a light breeze turned the twin brick chimneys into flutes, playing a tuneless melody.

She slid out of her satin sheets and wrapped her nude body in a brocaded silk robe. Then she climbed up the ladder to the widow's walk as she did every morning, throwing back the hatch to emerge in low, bright sunlight.

The sky was almost clear except for some low cumulus building to the north, but with the breeze out of the southwest, the sky would soon be perfectly clear, a rare phenomenon for this part of Maine.

First day of school. Her first encounter with

Lucas, no doubt. The first chance to observe how Zoey and the others would react. Had she and Jake succeeded in isolating Lucas?

"Is that really so important?" she asked herself. A fragment of dream nagged at her consciousness, but when she tried to recall it, it slipped away.

"Why is it so important?"

She tried to remember Lucas, the way she had known him. She tried to imagine the ways he might have changed in two years' time. And how she would feel when she saw him.

Was that it? Was it that she was afraid she might still care for him? Was that the reason she felt so compelled to push him away?

Maybe. Yes, maybe that was part of it.

And what was the rest of it? Claire asked herself. That was the question. In the meantime, she would follow her instincts.

And eventually things would work out the way she wanted. They almost always did.

"What, what?" Aisha woke up startled, eyes wide.

Her little brother, Kalif, was smirking down at her. "Mom said to wake you up."

"So you scream *the house is on fire*?"

"I tried whispering *wake up*, but it didn't work," Kalif said, heading out the door.

Aisha looked at the clock. The alarm must not be working. No, she'd forgotten to set it. But good old Mom had remembered. Thanks a lot, good old Mom.

She stumbled to her closet, found her robe, and put it on over the new bottle-green pajamas she'd worn to bed.

"Shower first or eat first?" she asked herself, pausing in the foyer. From the kitchen came the smell of coffee and her mother's fresh-baked muffins.

Well, if she ran late, would she rather show up at school hungry or dirty?

The first day of school was always such a fashion show, everyone trying to establish themselves. No one would know if she was starving. Everyone would notice if her hair was sticking out on one side of her head.

She sighed. Shower it was; food could wait.

"Welcome to the jun-gle, we got fun and ga-ames . . ."

"Guns," Jake said. "Good start to the day." His covers were already off, lying in a twisted pile by the foot of the bed, as usual.

He did a sit-up, stretching down to touch his toes, then rolled out of bed. He stretched, right arm arcing up over his head to a count of forty, then did the other arm. Then, bending at the waist, pulled his forehead against his left knee, counted to twenty-five, and the same on the right side.

He did twenty-five push-ups, fifty stomach crunches, and several more stretches.

Then he stood up and took a look at himself in the full-length mirror on his closet door. He flexed a bicep, looking at the result critically. Then he slapped his ridged, flat stomach, satisfied with the muscle tone.

Yes, he'd have no trouble making the football team again this year. He hadn't let himself go over the summer, like a lot of guys.

He glanced at the clock. The stretches and exercises had taken nearly ten minutes. It was six thirty-four. No time for a run this morning. He'd have to work on getting up half an hour earlier.

Lucas had been up since six. Six A.M. had been wake-up at the youth authority. Five minutes to get your act together, grab your soap and towel before they marched you down to the showers, where you confronted the unappetizing sight of several dozen naked guys. And if that didn't ruin your appetite, the food, usually runny scrambled eggs and fatty ham, would.

He leaned against the railing of his deck, a cup of delicious coffee in his hand, steam curling up, the aroma intoxicating. The air was fresh scrubbed, salty and clear, just some low clouds to the north, nowhere near obscuring the sun as it rose from behind the ridge.

The town below was all sharp morning shadows and gold-drenched brick and clapboard. The sun turned the church spire into a brilliant gold needle. Through the trees and building clutter he could just see a slice of the harbor, his father's trawler chugging around the point, heading for the patch of water where he set his lobster traps.

Closer at hand, he could see Mrs. Passmore at the sink in her kitchen, dumping the seeds from a cantaloupe. He longed to see Zoey wander in wearing that nightshirt of hers. It would be nice to go down for another breakfast with her, but school started today. She'd have enough on her mind.

He certainly had enough on his.

"You know, Nina, you're not going to be able to do that in class," Zoey said, indicating the unlit cigarette in Nina's mouth.

"Why not? It's only against the rules to *smoke* cigarettes."

"That's like saying it's only against the rules if you *shoot* heroin, Ninny," Jake said.

"Or *fire* a gun," Zoey added.

"Or *spend* money after you steal it," Aisha offered.

Nina shook her head glumly. "Here it is. Officially our first pointless discussion on the way to school of the season."

They gathered on the right side of the ferry, back toward the stern where they had always gathered last school year, and the year before that. It was the place. From there they could watch all the other passengers on the upper deck, stay out of the line of sight of Skipper Too and the bridge, and get the best view of Weymouth as they came in, right down to the flagpole in front of their school at the end of Mainsail Street.

Mr. Gray, Aisha's father, and Mr. Geiger, Claire and Nina's father, were down below, where, by custom, they stayed out of the way of their kids, reading their papers and drinking coffee from steel thermos bottles.

Claire leaned against the stern rail, gazing off toward the bank of clouds to the north. Zoey knew she'd long had a fixation of sorts for weather phenomena. Not that Claire ever really spoke of it. She just spent a lot of her time gazing at clouds, referring to them not just as clouds but as *cirrus* or *cumulonimbus*. Nina said she often sat up on her widow's walk in the middle of storms. It was a strange fascination, but then, Claire was a strange girl. She

172

was a friend, Zoey supposed, and yet there was always something a little withdrawn, a little preoccupied about Claire. Especially lately.

"Damn. There he is," Jake said, gritting his teeth.

Zoey didn't have to ask whom he was talking about. Lucas had come up the stairs to the upper deck. He looked in the direction of the group, turned away, and sat down toward the front, out of earshot but impossible not to see.

Had his gaze focused on her? Zoey wondered. Certainly not so anyone would notice.

Jake put his arm around her shoulders, drawing her to him. "I wasn't sure he'd have the nerve," he said.

"He has to go to school," Nina said. "How else is he going to get there?"

"He can swim," Jake said.

"Aren't you going to rush right up and beat the hell out of him?" Benjamin asked from the bench behind them.

Jake scowled. "I get into a fight and I could screw up my eligibility for the team."

Benjamin laughed. "Isn't that the reason the Swiss are always giving for staying out of wars? They don't want to screw up their chances of making the team."

"Come on, babe," Jake said, standing up and pulling Zoey to her feet.

"Where?"

"I want to stretch my legs," Jake said.

Zoey glanced nervously in Lucas's direction, but his back was turned to them. Reluctantly she fell in beside Jake as he walked slowly down the aisle toward the front of the boat.

"Jake, don't start anything. You know Benjamin was just trying to goad you."

"I'm not starting anything," Jake said. "I'm just taking a little walk around the deck."

Jake kept his arm around her shoulders and she could feel the tension in his muscles. Unfortunately, they were already so near Lucas that he would be sure to overhear if she argued with Jake anymore.

Nevertheless, she whispered through her teeth, "Jake, this is stupid."

"What? What are you talking about?" Jake said in a bad parody of innocence.

He turned and crossed in front of Lucas, Zoey still almost a prisoner in his strong grasp. Lucas's long legs were stretched out in front of him, and he slouched into the collar of his jacket, staring fixedly down toward the bow of the boat as it sliced through the water.

"You want to move your feet?" Jake said, his voice deadened.

Lucas slowly pulled his legs back, never looking up at Jake.

"Thanks, killer," Jake said. He turned his back on Lucas and leaned against the railing. Then he bent low and, to Zoey's amazement, kissed her on the lips. She pulled back in surprise.

Jake's eyes flared angrily, but she could tell he didn't want to say anything in front of Lucas.

"Let's go sit down, Jake," Zoey said tersely.

"No, I like it up here," he said, waving his arm expansively. "Up here I can look out and see the water. Sitting back there I found my view was obstructed by a piece of garbage. I hate looking at garbage, don't you, Zoey?"

Zoey shot a glance at Lucas, who was still sitting, staring calmly at nothing. Was Jake trying to pick a fight or just showing off?

Jake leaned his back to the railing, releasing Zoey. He stared straight down at Lucas. "I don't think Zoey likes garbage, either. I don't think anyone on the island likes garbage. You hear me, killer?"

Lucas took a deep breath and let it out slowly. "If you have a problem with me, Jake, don't drag Zoey into the middle of it."

"In the middle?" Jake demanded. "No, she's not in the middle. No one's in the middle. See, there's all of us on one side, and then there's you on the other, killer."

With a look of resignation, Lucas got to his feet. "Go ahead, Jake. Get it out of your system.

You want to take a shot at me? Fine. Here's your chance."

Before Zoey could open her mouth, Jake's fist flew through the air, catching Lucas in the stomach and doubling him over. A second blow caught the side of his face and knocked him down onto the steel deck.

"Cut that out!" Skipper Too's angry voice blasted from the P.A. system.

Jake danced back on his toes, fists ready, daring Lucas to get up.

And somehow, before she knew what she was doing, Zoey was on her knees, wrapping protective arms around Lucas's hunched back.

"Get away from him!" Jake roared. "He had it coming."

"Don't do this, Zoey," Lucas whispered, gasping for air.

Aisha and Nina rushed forward to grab Jake's arms and pull him back.

Zoey dug in her ferry bag for her little packet of Kleenex, pulled them all out, and pressed the wad against the flow of blood from Lucas's nose.

Skipper Too appeared, shoving Jake back and shouting, "I'll ban you from this boat, Jake, damned if I won't, if you don't get back there and sit down."

"That son of a bitch killed my brother!" Jake yelled hotly.

"I said sit down! By God, I'm the captain on this tub and you'll do what I tell you."

Jake backed away several feet. "Come on, Zoey. Leave that creep to bleed."

"Oh, shut up, Jake. Shut up!" Zoey cried.

"Go," Lucas said, trying to push her away. "Don't be stupid. I'm fine. I've taken worse."

"Zoey, damn it!" Jake yelled.

Zoey helped Lucas back to a sitting position, dabbing at him with her Kleenex in a vain attempt to keep the blood from staining his shirt. She could see Jake storming back to the others, shooting bitter looks of betrayal at her. Aisha and Nina seemed stunned, uncertain what to do as they stood halfway between Jake and Zoey.

As Zoey watched, Claire reached out and let her fingers settle on Jake's arm. Then her hand curled around his arm. It could have been a gesture of support, or comfort, or . . .

It all happened so quickly. No time to think. And now she knelt at Lucas's side, feeling very, very far away from the only friends she had.

Thirteen

"All right, line up, girls," Coach Anders said, giving a blast on her whistle that made Aisha wince. "Line up here on the sidelines. That's right. No, a *line,* not a gaggle."

Aisha jostled Zoey, who was on her left. "No gaggling," Aisha said under her breath, trying to get Zoey to laugh. Zoey could only manage a wan smile. Not that Aisha expected more, after the terrible scene on the morning ferry.

Aisha had handled that badly, she felt. She should have gone to Zoey, shown her some support. Zoey had looked so stricken and abandoned. And it wasn't like Aisha was on Jake's side.

Of course she wasn't on Lucas's either.

Why were there suddenly sides, anyway? Zoey was going to have to patch this up with Jake and quit feeling sorry for Lucas or it was going to put Aisha in a difficult spot.

"We are going to get right into it this year," Coach Anders announced, taking wide, swaggering steps along the line of girls in their gym shorts and Weymouth High T-shirts. "This," she held up a white-and-black ball, "is a soccer ball."

The class groaned in unison. Across the soccer field, a class of guys was running, one after another, toward a high jump, and, one after another, knocking the crossbar down.

"I know, you think because you're seniors you shouldn't even have to take gym class. Or else you think maybe it should just be aerobics or some such thing. Wrong." She stopped, dropped the ball to the grass, and put her foot on it. "Now, the school board did not approve my proposal to get you girls into weight training, but this will be just as tough."

"Oh, good," Aisha said under her breath. "It's important to be sweaty and bruised by the end of third period."

"Did you have something to add, Ms. Gray?" Coach Anders demanded.

"No, ma'am."

"Fundamentals!" Coach Anders shouted. "It's a game of fun-da-men-tals. And we are going to work on those fundamentals again and again until every woman here can thread this little ball through a field of opponents, get within scoring distance, and nail that goal."

A collective sigh of depression went through the group.

"Now, where are my balls?" Coach Anders demanded, looking down the field toward the gym.

Aisha snorted. Several girls giggled. Even Zoey cracked a smile.

Their coach's eyes flashed angrily, but she showed no sign that she understood what was funny. "There we go," she said, nodding in satisfaction. "Come on. Let's get moving!"

"Sorry, Coach, but one of them had a leak and I had to put on a patch."

Why was that voice familiar? Aisha wondered. She turned to look, but her view was blocked by Claire and several of the other girls.

"Women," Coach Anders announced, "meet our new equipment manager."

He ran up, wearing black bike shorts and a rugby shirt, carrying a large sack of balls slung over his shoulder.

"His name is Christopher Shupe. He'll be taking care of the balls, bats, nets, and so on. Mr. Forbes, who you may remember from last year, has moved to Florida."

"Hi," Christopher said, waving his hand to everyone and grinning directly at Aisha.

"It's a nightmare," Aisha muttered wonderingly. "Everywhere I go, there he is."

"Christopher was also on his high school varsity soccer team," Coach Anders went on, "so he's going to help us out with a few pointers."

Of course, Aisha thought darkly.

"Chris, why don't you pick out a volunteer, and we'll demonstrate some of the fun-da-men-tals."

Gee, I can't even begin to guess who he's going to choose, Aisha thought sarcastically. After all, the entire world, including her own mother and her gym teacher, was conspiring to get them together.

Christopher sent her a dazzling grin, then walked up, pointed his finger, and said, "All right, I sort of know Zoey, here. Maybe she'll give me a hand."

Zoey?

"Um, I'm really not . . . you know, very sporty," Zoey said lamely. "Wouldn't you like to get Aisha?"

Christopher shook his head. "No. No insult intended, but Aisha has somewhat large feet. I'm worried she might trip over herself."

Aisha felt her jaw drop open. She snapped it shut. *Somewhat large feet?*

"I'd never noticed before," Coach Anders said, looking down thoughtfully at Aisha's feet.

"I wear size nine," Aisha cried in protest. "That is not large!" Well, maybe nine and a half, but still . . .

"Nothing to be ashamed of," Coach Anders said heartily.

"I don't have big feet," Aisha repeated. "This is amazing. The first day of school and I'm being insulted. I can play soccer as well as anyone here."

"Are you interested in playing soccer?" Christopher asked. "Because desire goes a long way, as I'm sure Coach Anders will agree."

"Desire is half the battle. The other half is fun-da-men-tals."

"I have the desire not to have people think I can't play soccer," Aisha said hotly.

"Great. We were thinking of putting together some intramural teams," Christopher continued. "You sound so enthusiastic, Aisha. Meet me after school—we'll get together and see if we can get this thing started."

"Excellent," Coach Anders said, nodding vigorously. "I know you two will get the ball rolling, so to speak. Ha, ha."

Christopher just smiled.

"I'm so glad we're back in school," Nina said, wrinkling her nose at the food on her tray. "I don't get nearly enough tamale pie in my life."

Zoey looked at her own tray. "Oh. Right."

"You need to snap out of it, Zo," Nina chided, leading them toward a table. "You're walking around in a trance."

"Sorry," Zoey said. "I guess I'm distracted."

Nina shrugged. "Guys fight all the time. If they were left on their own, that's all they'd do. Don't take it so seriously."

They found an empty table, round with four orange plastic chairs. "It's not the fight, Nina. It's the fact that Jake thinks I betrayed him."

"I'm not eating this," Nina said. "These people need to make some kind of arrangement for those of us who don't eat dead cow. Jake will get over it."

"You really think so?"

"Well, not if you keep being nice to Lucas. But if what you want is to keep things together with Jake, you have to make a choice."

"Jake picked that fight," Zoey said.

Nina picked at the fruit cocktail on her tray. "Isn't it supposed to be *my boyfriend, right or wrong*?"

Aisha dropped into one of the vacant chairs. "Did you see what happened in gym class?" she demanded of Zoey. "That jerk played me like a fiddle."

"Like a fiddle?" Nina echoed, shaking her head disapprovingly.

"Okay, like whatever. He totally manipulated the situation. Zoey will tell you."

"Zoey, what's Aisha talking about?" Nina asked.

"Christopher," Aisha answered angrily. "How

many jobs does he have, anyway? Now Toni LaMara is calling me *Big Foot*. That's the kind of thing you don't want getting started. I told her I'd spread the rumor she slept with George Amos."

"Toni slept with George Amos?" Nina asked.

"No, of course not. Eew," Aisha said. "Don't gross me out. But she won't be calling me Big Foot again anytime soon."

"I guess this is some of that ultrasophisticated, worldly-wise stuff you seniors understand," Nina said.

Aisha hooked a thumb at Zoey. "She still depressed?"

"I'm not depressed," Zoey said. "Not exactly. I'm just trying to figure out what to do."

Aisha shrugged. "You have to pick a side and stay there. Which one do you want, Jake or Lucas?"

"It's not that easy," Zoey said.

"*Joke* has more muscles," Nina said. "Especially between his ears."

"But Lucas is kind of sexy," Aisha reflected.

"He's done time, Eesh. He's a guy who's had a mug shot, and probably had a number stenciled on his clothes. He probably has a tattoo that says *Born to Raise Hell* on his chest," Nina said. "No, he's more Claire's type."

"He's not good enough for your best friend,

but he'd be just fine for your sister?" Aisha said, laughing.

"They used to be tight, don't forget. Besides, it would be so much fun if Claire brought Lucas home to meet our dad. He loves Benjamin. He wants to pay Benjamin's way through college. He'd chew porcelain if he thought Lucas was going out with his precious Claire."

"Hmm. Then Benjamin would be free, I could ask him out, and that would so blow Christopher away," Aisha said.

"You and Benjamin? No way. Incompatible," Nina said dismissively. "Totally wrong."

"I can't believe I took Lucas's side against Jake," Zoey said shaking her head.

"Your nurturing instinct just took over. Apologize to Jake, blow off Lucas, get on with your life," Nina said.

"Tell Jake you can't stand the sight of blood, so you just lost it when he punched Lucas," Aisha advised. "He'll believe that. Besides, you two have to work it out; you're one of the Solid Couples."

"Really," Nina agreed. "You and Jake are pillars of Weymouth High society. People count on you. You're the very stable, slightly boring couple that other couples look to and say, Gee, why can't we have the kind of dull, predictable relationship Jake and Zoey have?"

Zoey smiled, in spite of the fact that she knew Nina was deliberately trying to goad her. "You're such a keen observer of other people's relationships, Nina. I guess it helps not to have one of your own to distract you."

Nina clapped a hand to her chest. "Ooh, straight through the heart."

"I'm not going to blow my relationship with Jake," Zoey said, trying to sound firm and decisive.

"I *am* going to blow my relationship with Christopher," Aisha said. "Whatever it takes. He cannot just barge his way into my life."

"I'm going to become a lonely, shriveled-up old lady," Nina said.

"Don't look," Aisha said urgently, leaning forward over the table. "It's Lucas."

"Is he coming this way?" Zoey asked, forcing herself to keep her gaze rigidly locked on Aisha.

"Yes. No. Wait a minute," Aisha said, throwing repeated glances across the crowded lunchroom.

"I'll call him over," Nina said.

"Nina!" Zoey cried.

"Kidding. Jeez, don't wet yourself."

"He's sitting down," Aisha said, leaning back with a sigh.

"I haven't seen Jake anywhere since homeroom," Zoey said.

"You'll see him on the ferry after school," Nina pointed out. "Just have a talk with him. He'll have his testosterone under control by then."

"He may not talk to me," Zoey said glumly.

"Then go to lip lock," Nina said.

Aisha nodded sagely. "Lip lock. That will do the trick."

"Slippery lippery."

"Mouth to mouth."

"Tongue twistage."

"Molar mining."

Zoey sighed. "I'm so glad I'm a senior now. Our conversations are so much more intelligent than they were last year."

Fourteen

To Zoey's surprise, neither Jake nor Lucas was on the four-o'clock ferry home. In fact, only Nina and Benjamin rode the ferry with her. Aisha had been roped into seeing Christopher about soccer. Claire, Zoey figured, could be waiting to take the water taxi home with her father. After all, they could afford it. Jake had probably decided to catch the later ferry, or arranged for his dad to pick him up in their boat.

As for Lucas, who knew? Zoey was not going to concern herself any further with Lucas Cabral. Jake was her boyfriend, and she owed him some loyalty and support. Obviously, this whole thing with Lucas had been difficult for him. She should have seen that and tried to help.

The trip home went peacefully, twenty-five minutes of gossip about the first day of school, teachers, classmates, and in Nina's case, a lengthy diatribe on the soul-crushing nature of school.

Zoey said good-bye to Nina and walked the rest of the way home with Benjamin.

"Nina said something about Mr. Geiger wanting to pay your way through college," Zoey said. "Or was she just exaggerating?"

Benjamin shrugged. "He did say that. I think he's hoping I'll marry Claire someday. He figures I'll be easier to control than some other potential sons-in-law."

"Doesn't that kind of piss you off?"

Benjamin smirked. "You think I'd really be easy to control?"

Zoey chuckled. "Not hardly."

"I don't take it seriously," Benjamin said.

When they reached the house, Zoey said a quick hello to her father, leaving him to cross-examine Benjamin about school, and went up to her room.

She sat down at her desk in the dormered window and closed her eyes. What a day. Not bad enough that it had been the first day of school, no, it had to start with a fight between her boyfriend and . . . some guy she barely knew.

Lucas. Why had she sided with Lucas? The obvious answer was because he wasn't the one who had started the fight, and he *was* the one who got hurt. That was the obvious answer. But was it the whole truth?

What *did* she feel for Lucas? And what did she feel for Jake?

She pulled out a yellow pad and wrote *JAKE*

at the top on the left side, *LUCAS* on the right. Then she drew a line down the middle of the page, creating two columns.

She thought for a moment, then, under the name *JAKE*, she wrote *Known him for years*. Since she was just a kid. He was the first guy ever to kiss her. He'd taught her to water ski. He had believed her when she'd denied the rumor going around that she was seeing Tad Crowley. (She'd only kissed Tad once at a party, that was it.)

Under *LUCAS* she wrote *Barely know him*. Strictly speaking, she'd known him since she was little, too. But he'd been away for two years. Things changed a lot in two years.

And then, not to be crude, but if you put the two of them side by side wearing little Speedos like those bodybuilders on ESPN, it would be no contest. And why shouldn't she think that way? Guys did.

Under *JAKE* she put *Great body*.

Not that Lucas had a bad body. Not at all. He was tall and lanky. He had long legs and broad shoulders. Seeing him in a Speedo wouldn't make her want to run screaming from the room or anything.

Under *LUCAS* she wrote *Okay body*.

So far, Jake was out in front. She went on, line after line, noting that Jake was a great kisser, while Lucas was an unknown in this category. You could hardly count that one little kiss two years earlier. He hadn't even moved his lips.

The further she went, the more obvious it was that Jake was totally superior in every category to Lucas.

After filling half the page, she wrote *Jake makes me feel* . . . She hesitated. What did Jake make her feel? She imagined the many, many times they had lain together, out on the beach by a blazing campfire, or just on the couch in the family room. She could feel his big arms wrapped around her, holding her close.

. . . *safe.* That's what Jake made her feel. Like nothing could ever harm her when she was in his arms.

And Lucas? *Makes me feel* . . . she wrote.

She remembered him on the breakwater, waves crashing around him. And she remembered the queasy, unsettled, disturbed feeling after he had lifted her hand to his lips.

She quickly crossed out the line. She added the fact that Jake clearly had a very excellent chest, all smooth, tan muscles, while Lucas probably had a tattoo there.

Then she looked down the list. It certainly was one sided. A person looking over this list would reach only one conclusion. Obviously, Jake was the right choice.

Still, maybe she had been slightly unfair to

Lucas. He did have better hair than Jake, in her opinion. Even so, it was no contest.

"Of course it isn't," she said aloud. "Jake is your boyfriend. Jake loves you. Jake does not have a tattoo."

She hid the pad in her drawer and stood up. She would go to Jake, apologize, make some good excuses, and then, as Nina and Aisha had suggested, go to lip lock.

And life would be back to normal.

Her eye settled on the Post-it note bearing the quote.

A man ^(or a woman) can stand almost anything except a succession of ordinary days.

She took it down and crumpled it, letting it drop in the wastebasket. What did Goethe know about life on Chatham Island?

The List

Jake	Lucas
-Known him for years	-Barely know him
-Great body	-Okay body
-Like his mom	-His dad is a little intense
-Very good kisser	-?
-Never got anyone killed	-Probably got someone killed
-Everyone likes him but Nina	-No one likes him
-Thinks he's going to marry me	-Says he thought of me a lot
-Getting kind of gropey	-Hasn't seen a girl in 2 years
-Friend as well as boyfriend	-Neither
-Makes me feel safe	~~-Makes me feel~~
-Excellent chest	-Possible tattoo?
-Don't like his hair	-Nice hair

*   *   *

"Yes, I did have an interesting dream," Claire admitted. She leaned back against the cool leather, enjoying the crackling sound it made. Dr. Kendall raised her eyebrow expectantly. Dr. Kendall loved dreams, Claire had discovered. Unfortunately, most weeks Claire had no dreams to tell her psychiatrist, at least none that she could remember.

"As usual, I don't remember it perfectly."

"Do the best you can."

Claire smiled coyly. "I'm afraid there's no kinky sex or anything in it."

Dr. Kendall just nodded. Claire knew this was because Dr. Kendall believed *everything* was something psychological. If Claire sat up straight, that meant something. If she slouched, that meant something, too. If she yawned, it couldn't just be that she was tired; no, it had to be something of a deep-seated psychological nature.

She'd been seeing the shrink since her mother had died. About the time of the accident her father suggested she might want to drop the sessions, but by that point Claire had gotten used to it. It was a familiar ritual, comforting, sort of like some people said church was.

"Well," Claire began. "It was in the car again."

"*The* car?"

"Uh-huh. Only it was a lobster. You know,

a four-wheeled lobster with a stick shift."

"Go on."

"Lucas was there. And Wade. And we were skidding around but laughing just the same. All three of us."

"Yes." Dr. Kendall nodded wisely.

"That's about it. Except that we started to crash, and Lucas was trying to grab the wheel out of my hand."

"Lucas was—"

"I mean, I was trying to grab the wheel away from him, only my hands were slippery."

"I see. And then?"

"Then we crashed. And I woke up." Suddenly an image flashed in Claire's mind. A sharp, clear picture. She shook her head angrily.

"Is there something else?"

"Nothing. Just that I suddenly had this weird flash of Benjamin, standing by the side of the road after we had crashed."

"Benjamin? This is your male friend, right? The unsighted one?"

"The blind guy, yeah. He was staring at us, very solemn, and it was his actual eyes, not his sunglasses. I mean, it's like in my dream he could see or something."

Dr. Kendall nodded.

"So?" Claire asked, dismissing the lingering

effects of the dream image. "So what's it all mean?"

"It could mean any number of things," Dr. Kendall said.

Claire rolled her eyes. Well, there you had it: the perfect shrink answer. "Come on, I have the kind of weird dream that my sister Nina has every night—and sometimes during the day—and it doesn't even mean anything?"

Dr. Kendall smiled her noncommittal smile. "Dream interpretation can be tricky. Perhaps you simply ate a lobster and remembered it in your dream."

"Actually, I did."

"There you go."

"Well, I'm disappointed. You ask me for dreams and I finally bring you one loaded up with twisted imagery, drivable lobsters the size of Volkswagens, blind guys who can see . . . I don't really think I can get much crazier than that."

"We don't use the word crazy, Claire. And in any event you are an extremely sane person. For your age, one might even say you're abnormally sane. Apart from the fact that you don't remember certain events surrounding the accident, you appear to be quite well adjusted. In fact, you show great self-awareness and excellent coping skills."

"Are you telling me I shouldn't keep coming?"

Dr. Kendall looked at her thoughtfully. "Claire, you may never remember. It may simply be physical, and not in any way psychological. You did suffer a concussion in the accident."

"Oh, I see."

"Certainly you can keep coming here, if you feel you need someone to talk to, if you're lonely."

"I'm not lonely," Claire said quickly, dismissively.

"No?"

"No. Of course not. I'm just . . . solitary. A loner."

"There's nothing wrong with being solitary," Dr. Kendall said with a reassuring smile. "Still, if you'd like to schedule another session for next week—"

Claire felt an unfamiliar pang of confusion and doubt. "Maybe I . . . maybe I should." Claire shrugged. "You know, sort of taper off slowly."

"We could make your next visit in *two* weeks."

"Okay." Claire stood up. "Well, I have to catch the ferry." She reached the door, then hesitated. "You know, though, if I come every two weeks, I'm bound to forget whether I'm supposed to come or not, so maybe we should just keep doing it every week. You know, just because it's easier."

Zoey walked from her house down to Dock Street where it ran along Town Beach, feeling nervous and a little annoyed for some indefinable reason. Yes, yes, she knew she had to go and work things out with Jake, but still, it was annoying. It wasn't like she'd committed some big crime.

From the point where Dock merged into Leeward Drive she could look up and see Jake's house, brightly lit so that even in the black of a moonless night, you could see the red of the cedar.

She walked on, the agitated waters of the bay on her right, a breeze rustling the pines on her left. High, thin clouds like gray lace scudded overhead. The skyline of Weymouth glittered brightly, the office buildings no doubt full of hardworking types catching up after the three-day weekend.

She climbed the twisting, steep driveway to Jake's house and cut along the well-known path around the side and down to the flagstone patio.

She peeked tentatively around the corner. After that last visit she didn't want any more sudden revelations. Through the sliding glass door she could see Jake, wearing only a pair of shorts, leaning back on his bed, watching TV and throwing a football up into the air while he tried to catch it with his left hand.

Standing there in the dark, she knew she was invisible.

"See?" Zoey reminded herself. "Great body."

She stepped forward into the pool of light and tapped on the glass. He looked at her, seemed to hesitate for a moment, and then, with a show of reluctance, got up and opened the door.

"Hi, Jake."

"Hi, Zoey," he said in a voice several degrees colder than hers.

"I thought we should talk."

"Do we have something to talk about?"

"I think we do," she said. She slid past him into the room. He closed the door behind her but remained standing, still holding his football, while she sat on the edge of his bed.

"Let me just get this out right away," Zoey said. She took a deep breath. "I'm sorry if what happened this morning made it seem like I was choosing sides against you."

"That's what it was," he said.

"No, it wasn't, Jake. I . . . I just can't stand violence. My first reaction was to help Lucas because he was hurt. I don't think that makes me a bad person," she added plaintively.

"He wasn't hurt," Jake growled. "If I'd really wanted to hurt him . . . well, I could have if I'd wanted to."

"His nose was bleeding," Zoey said.

"He had it coming."

Zoey suppressed an urge to point out that it was Jake who had picked the fight. That wouldn't help. "I'm sorry," she said.

"I thought you were—" To Zoey's amazement, Jake's voice actually broke. "I thought you were, like, being interested in him. You know?"

"You mean as in *romantic* interest?" Zoey said, loading her voice with disbelieving surprise. "Lucas?"

Jake made a wry, embarrassed grin. "Maybe I was just imagining things."

"You were jealous?" Zoey said a little shrilly.

Jake shrugged. "I was kind of upset at the time."

Zoey got up from the bed and crossed the room. He waited for her to come, offering no overt encouragement. She put her hand on his arm.

"Jake, you and I have been together forever. We're a couple. Today at lunch Nina said we're the couple everyone looks up to."

"Ninny said that?" he asked skeptically.

"Well, something like that," Zoey admitted, grinning.

Jake smiled back. "I can just imagine what she really said." Then his face grew somber again. "It's just, look, I love you. You know that."

"Yes, I do," Zoey said softly.

"I have to be sure you're on my side."

Zoey nodded. "Of course I am. Just don't go around getting into fights. You'll get in trouble."

"Okay. Deal. No more fights."

He slipped his arm around her waist and pulled her to him. She responded, entwining herself around him, opening her mouth to accept his kiss.

It felt wonderful. It felt as if the world that had been torn was now neatly sewed up. Life was back to normal, things once again as they ought to be.

Draft #24

. . . and with a roar, the
white Knight swung his
gleaming broadsword, shat-
tering the shield in Sir
Luke's hand and Knocking
him to the ground.

"I yield!" Sir Luke cried,
holding up his arm as if
to ward off the final blow.

"Yield?" the white Knight
roared. "You are no gentle-
man, whatever your title. You
have no honor, and thus
I give you no mercy." He
raised the broadsword high
over his head. "For all the
suffering you have inflicted
on the peasants, and for
your base treason, I send
you straight to hell!"

"No!" Raven cried, gathering her skirts and rushing to the fallen Sir Luke. She spread her arms, shielding the villain, though she well knew the terrible suffering he had inflicted on the people.

"What?" the white knight cried. "You would protect this knave?"

"Nay," Raven cried just as fiercely, "it is you I protect. The king has ordered that this foul creature, though his sins are ~~manifest~~ manifold many, should be taken alive."

"Out of my way, woman. My vengeance will not be delayed."

"Stay your hand, my lord,"

Raven said. "If you strike, you will make yourself as base as this evildoer. You must obey the King!"

"I care not for reason!" The white knight raised his sword higher still. "Stand aside, Raven, and let him meet the devil, his master!"

Raven threw her arms tightly around the cringing shoulders of Sir Luke. "If you strike him, you will destroy me as well."

The white knight's eyes blazed. But Raven knew his love was even greater than his rage. Slowly he lowered the sword till its point was in the dust. Then, with a quick, decisive thrust, the white Knight sheathed his sword. "I thank you, fair maiden, for you have kept me from committing a grave error in my righteous rage."

Sir Luke breathed a sigh of relief. "You saved my life," he told Raven.

"Nay," she said, "for your judgment still awaits at the hand of the King."

~~"Nevertheless," Sir Luke said. He raised her hand to his lips. Raven felt~~

Fifteen

"Several announcements this morning," came the gravelly voice of the principal, Mr. Hardcastle. "Several announcements, if I may have everyone's attention, please."

Zoey caught Aisha's attention and rolled her eyes at the P.A. Homeroom lasted fifteen minutes and came just before the first lunch. By this point in the day, everyone was hungry, and no one wanted to hear Mr. Hardcastle go on about rules, regulations, meetings, events, rallies, and the other stuff he went on and on and on about every day.

To make matters worse, the day before, Ms. Lambert, their homeroom teacher, had demonstrated the annoying habit of taking all the announcements seriously and actually asking them questions afterward to see if they had paid attention. Ms. Lambert was new, of course, this being her very first class. Sooner or later she'd learn to chill a little.

". . . a matter has come up that requires

some clarification," Mr. Hardcastle said. "It is against school policy to allow students to smoke cigarettes on campus. This policy applies whether or not the student actually *lights* the cigarette."

Zoey and Aisha exchanged a look and laughed. Zoey scribbled a quick note on her pad, tore off the slip of paper, and when she was sure Ms. Lambert was looking away, started it on its way from hand to hand toward Aisha. The note said,

Nina will be thrilled.
She'll think she's a
celebrity.

". . . although as far as we know, an *unlit* cigarette does not pose a health hazard, we feel it is important to be consistent in enforcing . . ."

Aisha received the note, read it, and scribbled one back. It changed hands three times before reaching Zoey:

Nina will be thrilled. She'll think she's a celebrity.

You know how Nina loves to provoke. Speaking of which, I was too busy doing homework on the ferry this a.m.; what happened with you and Jake? Kiss and make up?

". . . turning to student government, and the fact that so far we have no nominations—no *serious* nominations—for any of the offices . . ."

Zoey glanced at Jake, in the back of the

room, looking like he might fall asleep and let his head crash onto the desk at any moment.

Slippery lippery, as you and Nina put it so maturely. All better now. How about you and <u>soccer</u> practice?

". . . include student council president, student council vice president, head of the school spirit committee, which is responsible for . . ."

Aisha grimaced as she read the last part of Zoey's note. She scribbled a long note and sent it back.

". . . and that concludes the morning announcements. Have a nice day."

The sound of a chair scraping the floor startled Zoey, coming in the sudden silence. "Well, *I* have an announcement to make," Ms. Lambert said, getting up from her desk and walking deliberately down the center aisle of the classroom. She stopped beside Bella Waterton and held out her hand. "I wish to announce that note passing is a no-no. A rather juvenile no-no for a class of seniors. Give it up, Ms. Waterton."

Bella shrugged apologetically at Aisha and handed the folded note to the teacher.

Ms. Lambert unfolded the note and read it over. She carried it back to her desk.

She wouldn't read it out loud, would she? Zoey wondered, aghast at the possibilities.

"My policy will be to read aloud any note I intercept in this class," Ms. Lambert said. "Homeroom is not just a time for you to play around." She held the note out at arm's length. *"Christopher is such a jerk to trap me into that. I'm going to kill him. I blew him off, even though it will probably piss Coach off. Although I will—"* Ms. Lambert blushed a little, suddenly appearing uncomfortable. But she took a breath and went on. *". . . although I will say he has a cute little butt, running around in those bike shorts."*

Aisha was sinking slowly under her seat as the room erupted in hoots and catcalls. Anyway, Zoey figured, Ms. Lambert had gotten a lesson in why it was a bad idea to read notes aloud.

"Zoey, wait up," Lucas said as the class poured out of last period and into the boisterous hallways.

Zoey pretended not to hear and kept walking, making a beeline for her locker. Then she felt a hand on her arm. She turned around, fixing an indignant look on her face.

"Look," Lucas said, "I know you're trying to avoid me and that's fine. I understand. I just stopped you to say that we don't have to pay any attention to what Mr. Bushnell said back there."

"I wasn't planning to," Zoey said. Mr. Bushnell taught French, and Lucas and she had the same class. The teacher had suggested that all the students form partnerships, with someone they saw regularly with whom they could converse in French. He'd suggested, for example, that since Zoey and Lucas were both island kids, they could speak to each other in French on the ferry rides to and from school.

This suggestion had caused Zoey to turn white. The idea that she would be gaily chattering away in *French* with Lucas while Jake sat a few feet away was a little hard to picture.

"Cool," Lucas said. He released her arm and seemed to sink back within himself.

"It's not—" Zoey began. *No, shut up, Zoey,*

she chided herself. So he looked like the loneliest human being on earth. That was not her problem. She had no interest in him.

After all, she had made a list.

"It's not that I'm trying to be a jerk," Zoey said lamely.

"I know," Lucas said.

"If it were up to me, sure, I'd be glad to . . . to talk French with you."

He grinned. *"C'est la vie."*

Zoey smiled back, glancing nervously down the hall for any sign of Jake. But of course he would be out on the field, getting in some practice for the football tryouts.

"Oui, c'est la vie, mais c'est . . . um, *c'est une bêtise, tout le même."* She made a face. "Did I say that right?"

"That's life, but it's dumb, just the same," he translated. "I'm not sure. It sounded right to me. But then, it's been two years since my last French class."

Zoey nodded. The reminder that he had been "away" for the last two years made her tense up. She really had to cut this off. Maybe she could go out to the field and watch Jake run. "I guess there's not a lot of French spoken at . . . at that place."

"It's not all that common, no," Lucas said.

An awkward silence descended. *I need to get*

out of here, Zoey reminded herself. *Maybe Jake's not around, but Claire might be, or even Nina or Aisha.*

"Was it really bad?" Zoey blurted. "The reform school?"

"YA. Youth Authority. Although we called it a few different things." He shrugged and looked away. "It wasn't Devil's Island or anything. The food was pretty bad."

Zoey smiled. "So, then, I guess cafeteria food must seem pretty okay?"

"Nothing could make the cafeteria food seem good," he said. "Still, you end up missing a lot of stuff while you're in there. Like pizza. Like McDonald's. The funny thing is, I was never all that crazy about McDonald's, but when you can't have a Big Mac and fries, they start to seem like the most important thing on earth. You lie in your rack at night thinking, Man, I've give anything for a Big Mac and fries."

"So did you run out first thing to Mickey D's?"

"Haven't been yet," Lucas admitted. "I've been on the island until yesterday. And yesterday after school I had to go see my caseworker. You know, have her tell me to stay off drugs and so on."

The hallway was emptying fast as kids piled out the doors, and the two of them, standing

213

there talking, were becoming ever more conspicuous. All it would take would be Jake coming in for a drink of water or something and there would be a major blowup. Even if it seemed rude, she had to get away.

"Well, I'll see you in class," Lucas said, turning away.

"Wait!" Zoey said. "Um, my parents' real car is in the lot down the street, and I have the keys, and we could maybe run out to the McDonald's by the mall and still get back in time for the ferry." Her face was flushed, her head was spinning, and her mouth was saying things she didn't want it to say.

"Zoey, you don't have to—"

"I'm hungry, that's all," Zoey said.

"I doubt anyone from school would be out there," Lucas reasoned. "I guess if they were, they'd be *in* the mall. But there is one other problem. I don't have any money."

"My treat." What was she thinking?

It took five minutes to arrive by back roads at the parking garage, and ten minutes to reach the restaurant. Lucas and Zoey decided by unspoken mutual agreement to eat in the car. As soon as they'd paid for a Big Mac, large fries, and a milk shake they drove out past the airport and away from town. There was still the chance that someone from school might show up in the restaurant itself. And the sight of Zoey Passmore sharing a milk shake with Lucas Cabral would instantly become *the* gossip the next day at school.

They listened to the radio and Lucas wolfed down the burger. He remarked from time to time on the sights—a new shopping center that hadn't been there the last time he'd driven this way, a new car model he had seen only on TV.

They joined the coast road, heading north through tall pines and flashes of rocky shore-line. Zoey found it strangely liberating. Off the island, away from school, she felt a delicious sensation of freedom. Sometimes it was a relief to be where nobody knew you, where your every action wouldn't become common knowl-edge within minutes.

"Pull in there." Lucas pointed with a french fry down a small, single-lane road.

Zoey turned so sharply that it threw Lucas against her. He apologized, and they both laughed nervously as he retrieved several spilled fries from her lap.

"Where are we going?" Zoey asked. The nar-row road forced her to slow down. Then, quite suddenly, it reached its end, a gravel patch be-yond which was nothing but wide sky and the ocean.

"Come on," he said, opening the door. "You'll like this."

She followed him across the gravel to the edge of the bluff. A hundred feet below them, the churning sea worked its slow, endless destruction on the rocks, relentlessly grinding them into sand. Sea gulls flew by at eye level, soaring on the wind that rose from the cliff. Across the water was Chatham Island, a dark mass dotted here and there with barely visible points of color and light.

"I can't believe I've never been down this road," Zoey said. "What a great view. The old island looks downright romantic from here."

"My father has his lobster pots ranged just out there." Lucas pointed down the coast. "The red markers with green stripes."

Zoey could see the familiar wooden floats that marked the locations of lobster traps. Lobstermen carved out territories, sometimes handed down through a dozen generations. Mr. Cabral had acquired this area from a cousin of his, an old Portuguese fisherman who had died twenty years earlier.

"Are you going to take over from your dad when he retires?" Zoey asked.

Lucas shook his head. "I think once he wanted me to, but I'd have to say it's pretty unlikely now. By mutual agreement."

"It's hard work," Zoey said.

"Yep."

They fell into silence. Zoey listened to the sounds of the gulls, the crash of water, the grinding of rocks, the far-off whistle of the ferry. Later she'd have to come up with some story for why she'd missed the four o'clock. Later. Right now she was far from prying eyes and hours away from excuses.

"Sorry," Lucas said. "Now I guess we're stuck till the six thirty."

"I don't mind," Zoey said. She smiled at him. "You have special sauce on your mouth."

He reached to wipe it off but missed. Zoey reached up and wiped his face.

"Thanks," he said softly.

"Uh-huh." She found she was staring at his lips. She found she was remembering the list she'd made, and the way she'd had to put a question mark under his name on the subject of kissing.

She found that they were standing closer, without either of them having moved.

And she found her heart thudding, so loud it was drowning out the cries of the gulls, and the crash of the water, and the grinding of the rocks.

His hand on her arm. Hers on his shoulder. Her eyes closing. His arm around her waist. Her breasts crushed against his chest. The feel of sinewy muscles in his back. His thigh and hers.

His lips on hers, soft, gentle, terrible urgency restrained. Her lips on his, trembling, surprised, uncertain.

Her mouth opening. And his.

Her fingers now entangled in his hair, unable to stop, just making things worse.

And sudden desire for more, knowing he wanted her, the unsettling realization that she wanted him as well.

Then withdrawal, both exerting control, both smiling sheepishly, and kissing again, more tentatively.

Well, Zoey thought, at least she could fill in the blank spot on her list.

Sixteen

From the front of the ferry Benjamin heard the sound of the heavy rope being cast off, slipping up the piling, and falling on the wooden slats of the dock. He had heard the feet of the crewman, running to the stern to cast off that line. He waited for the shriek of the whistle.

It sounded.

So. No Zoey. She would have come over to say hello.

Beside him he felt Claire's arm strain as she turned to scan the deck. What did she see? Not Zoey. Lucas? No, not Lucas, either, because whatever she was looking at had caused her to relax.

So, no Zoey and no Lucas. Interesting.

And Jake? Yes, Jake, that's who she was looking at, he was almost sure. She wouldn't spend this long focusing on Aisha. That left Jake, and now she was tilting her head slightly, a movement that translated as her shoulder pulling away.

"What's the weather like?" Benjamin asked.

219

"Oh, it's nice, a little overcast."

Yes, she was staring at Jake, and thinking about him. Claire never gave an answer about weather as simple as *a little overcast*.

The ferry was pulling away now, backing into a turn to head toward the bay. He could feel the heat of the afternoon sun, slowly moving from his face, to the side of his face, to the back of his neck, until the ferry was pointed out to sea.

"I have to run down to the girls' room," Claire said.

A lie. "It's called a *head* on a boat," Benjamin said.

So, she was going to talk to Jake. And she didn't want him to know. How interesting. Of course Claire would have noticed that neither Zoey nor Lucas was on the ferry. And if Jake hadn't noticed, or if he hadn't become suspicious on his own, Claire was going to plant the seed.

He strained to hear their conversation. They were far away, and the boat throbbed and vibrated, obliterating much sound. Still, he could hear snatches. It wasn't that blind people's hearing was any more acute, as he'd explained to Claire, it was just that without the distraction of sight they could concentrate much more intensely on hearing.

It wasn't Claire he could hear, though. Her voice was soft. Jake, fortunately, had a voice that carried well.

". . . last night, I mean . . . fine now, we talked . . . way . . . maybe she . . . shopping with Nina. Oh. I didn't see Ninny over . . ."

Oh, so Nina was on the ferry, Benjamin noted. And yet she hadn't come over to say hello, to him or to her sister. Well, Nina could be moody at times.

". . . Lucas? How would I know? . . . yeah . . . back in jail . . . I'm just not the suspicious . . . uh-huh . . . not worried . . . okay . . . sure . . . about Benjamin? . . . I guess, sure . . ."

Benjamin kept his face blank. He heard Claire approaching, the familiar sound of her walk, the smell of her perfume, her shampoo.

"Sorry. There was a line." Claire lied smoothly.

"Women's bathrooms are always that way," Benjamin said. *Just what game are you playing, Claire?* he asked silently. *What game? And do you even know you're playing it?*

"Is Nina around?" Benjamin asked.

"Yes. You want me to call her over?"

"No. I just wanted to set something up for some homework reading. Where is she?"

"Um, last bench, over on the other side."

"Thanks. I'll be right back," Benjamin said. He stood, turned a sharp left, checking with his left hand for the end of the bench. He counted the steps, reached for and found the railing, then followed it right.

"Nina?" he said when he knew he was close.

"Hi, Benjamin," she said. Her voice sounded just slightly sulky.

He sat beside her. "Is Jake nearby?" he asked in a low voice.

"No," she said, dropping to a conspiratorial whisper. "He's up at the front. Why?"

"Just wondering. It's nice to know who's listening when you talk to someone."

"I guess so."

"Look, Nina, you and I are friends, right?" Benjamin said.

"Um, sure." Her voice was a little strained.

"You know I hate to ask anyone anything. I mean, unless it's something I just can't do myself."

"Sure."

"Well, this is something kind of embarrassing, so if you don't want to answer, don't. It's just that I can only do so much without being able to see. I have a question, like I said, an embarrassing question."

"I'll do my best," Nina said doubtfully.

"Just now Claire was talking to Jake, wasn't she?"

"Uh-huh." A guarded answer, like she was hiding something.

"She's with him right now, again, isn't she?"

"Kind of."

"Well, maybe that answers my question," Benjamin said, muttering darkly.

"What question?"

He sighed. Even with eyes, it was hard to see into a person's heart. "Look, is Claire . . . is she, you know, interested in Jake?"

Nina was silent. He could feel her staring across the deck.

"She's never said anything," Nina said evenly.

"Okay, okay," Benjamin said, letting his frustration show, "but right now, as you look at them, as you *see* them talking, as you see them making eye contact or not, touching or not touching, sitting close or keeping their distance: Is she interested in him?"

"Jeez, Benjamin," Nina said.

He waved his hand, annoyed at his display of frustration. "Never mind. Forget it, Nina. I was just—"

"Yes," Nina said, blurting the word out. "She is."

He sat back down. "Damn."

"I mean, that's how it looks to me, anyway, not that I would know."

"Damn," he repeated softly. "Why?"

"I have no idea. I never really saw why Zoey liked him, either. Claire's always said he's good-looking, but I never thought she was interested, you know?" Nina said, sounding as if she were thinking out loud. "But then, who knows? I mean, I guess sometimes a girl suddenly looks at someone she's known a long time and all of a sudden, well, he seems different to her. Or maybe she's the one who changed. Maybe the guy . . . maybe he doesn't even realize she's interested or anything."

"Yeah," he said flatly. "She'll make sure he knows."

"Maybe she's shy," Nina said very softly.

"What? Claire, shy?" Benjamin said derisively. No, she wasn't shy. Not really. Not when she wanted something or someone. And now, suddenly, it seemed she wanted Jake. Why? Because she suspected Zoey might be releasing him? Or was it just that she was tired of being with a guy who couldn't even tell her she was beautiful?

Well, fine. He didn't care. He'd known it would end eventually.

"Thanks, Nina," he said. "I guess."

"Yeah, right," she said, sounding angry. Probably Nina didn't appreciate being used as a spy, although she should have a little concern for him. It was his feelings that were being trampled, not hers. He was the one left looking like a fool.

*   *   *

"Troll. Maggot. Tweedledum *and* Tweedle-dumber." Nina raged around her room, kicking aside piles of clothing on the floor, throwing her arms wide, then clapping them on her hips. "Blind? Blind isn't half of it. If he could see, he'd still be blind. He's sputum. He's a bad odor. He's a stain!"

What did it take, anyway? She'd been pretty obvious. It wasn't like Benjamin was incapable of grasping subtleties, the jerk. He could figure out someone's entire life history after hearing them say three words. But oh, when it came to her, well, *then* he was utterly impervious. Blank. Blank squared. Duh to the tenth power.

"It's not like I'm asking all that much," she said to a poster of Axl Rose. "I'm not talking ravishment here. I'm not saying, Hey, let's move immediately to a Condition of Maximum Erogenization. It's just that he's like the first guy in my whole life I ever thought, Yes, yes, I could steam some glass with this guy. The stinking scab."

Okay, so he was going out with her sister. Sure. But she didn't love him and he didn't love her.

Did he?

How could he? How could he love Claire, the ice queen, a girl who could make Shannen Doherty take a step back and say, *Whoa, that girl's a real bitch.*

After all, it wasn't as if Benjamin could be transfixed by her beauty. He was the one guy around who couldn't be, which should mean that he could concentrate on inner beauty, soul, heart, conscience, sensitivity. And what with Claire having *E: none of the above*, it should be an open-and-shut case.

No way he could really be in love with her. Especially now, with her licking her lips for Jake.

"And what's that all about?" she asked Axl suspiciously. Just Claire's usual need to be drooled over by every male over the age of nine?

There was a knock at her bedroom door. "Nina? Are you talking to someone in there?" Claire called through the door.

"I'm having a psychotic break and talking to the voices in my head!" Nina yelled.

"Oh. Just the usual. Zoey's on the phone."

Nina stomped to the door and threw it open.

"I'll hang up downstairs as soon as you pick this phone up," Claire said, trotting down the stairs.

Nina snatched up the phone in the hallway. "Zo?"

"It's me. Is Claire around?"

"I thought you wanted to talk to me," Nina said a little crossly.

"I do, and I don't want her listening in."

"Claire!" Nina yelled down the stairs. "I got it. You can hang up the phone now." In the receiver she heard the scuffling clatter of the other extension being hung up. "Okay, spill. What's the secret?"

"I'm still in Weymouth. I just wanted to know if Jake took the four o'clock with you guys."

"You just need to know that, huh?"

"Yes. Was he on the ferry or not?"

"You're going to have to do better than that, Zoey." Nina glanced left and right down the hallway. "Come on, come on. This has something to do with . . . with *L*, doesn't it?"

Zoey's end of the line was silent.

"*He* wasn't on the four o'clock," Nina said. "You and *L*, neither of you was on the four o'clock."

"Damn."

"You think I wouldn't notice a little coincidence like that?" Nina said.

"How about Jake?"

"I'll tell if you tell."

"You first."

"He *was* there, so if what you want to know is whether it will be safe for you and *L* to take the next one home without being seen, the answer is yes," Nina said quickly. "However—"

"However?"

"However," Nina continued, "I think I can guarantee that your absence was not unnoticed by certain people, initials *J* and *C*."

A heavy sigh.

"So. Now it's your turn," Nina said. "What have you been doing?"

"(mumble) went for a drive."

"Excuse me? Who went for a drive?"

"Just felt like going for a drive," Zoey said.

"Who. Not why, who?"

Another sigh. "Swear to me on a stack of Bibles."

"You and Luc—you and *L*?"

"He wanted a Big Mac."

"Right. He wanted a Big Mac," Nina sneered.

"Really. That's what he wanted."

"Yeah? And what did he *get*?"

"Don't be crude."

"Oh, my God, did he try to kiss you?" Nina's mind went into overdrive. Zoey and Lucas? *Oh, my God.* That would mean sooner or later Jake would find out. Then, what would keep him from going to Claire? And then, Benjamin would be free! Unless Claire lost interest in Jake as soon as he was truly available. Claire was capable of that.

Suddenly she realized Zoey hadn't answered. "Zoey?"

"Yes."

"You kissed him, didn't you?"

"Kind of."

"You slut. Do you realize what this will mean? What about Jake? What about the fact that Lucas is a jailbird?" *What about Benjamin?* she added silently. "The entire structure of our lives is going to crumble now because you wanted to fool around with Lucas."

"The entire structure of our lives?" Zoey repeated incredulously.

"Not to be unkind here, Zo, but look at what Lucas did to the entire structure of Wade's life."

"Nina, stop it!" Zoey ordered. "Maybe it's not as simple as that. Maybe Benjamin really is on to something."

"What? Zoey, *what* are you talking about?" Nina asked crossly.

"About the accident. About how the car was a little Volkswagen and there were only two seats in front. You remember," Zoey went on in a rush.

"I remember," Nina said. "Well, you know something? Benjamin isn't exactly Sherlock Holmes sometimes. As my dad pointed out, Lucas pleaded guilty, so there wasn't much point in asking questions about who was in what seat. We all know who was driving and what happened."

"You told your dad?"

Nina stiffened a little, feeling defensive. It

wasn't very often she had anything to say that would interest her father in the slightest. And this had. "It just came up, all right? I didn't think it was a big secret or anything."

"Well, *this* is a big secret, just so you know."

"I'll wait for you at the dock. I will require details, full, complete details."

"Just keep your mouth shut, all right?"

"Locked. Sealed. Crazy glued," Nina vowed.

Zoey hung up the phone. Nina settled the receiver back in its cradle, but just as she pulled it away from her ear, she heard a second soft but unmistakable click.

Seventeen

Claire backed away from the phone, staring at it as if it were a snake ready to strike. Already she could hear Nina coming down the steps.

"Claire! You weasel, were you listening in?"

Claire backed through the living room into the dining room just as Nina reached the bottom of the stairs and burst into the living room.

"I guess not," she heard Nina say.

Claire ducked quickly out the sliding glass doors that led from the dining room onto the patio.

It was a lot to digest all at once. Too much. Zoey falling for Lucas, that was bad.

Not that Claire could deny Lucas's attraction. Yes, she remembered that about him, the way he could make your insides melt with a look or a touch. And now he had broken the solid wall of resistance. Now it would be infinitely harder to get rid of him.

And then there was Benjamin's little theory. What was that all about? Some question about who was driving the car? What did Benjamin suspect, that *Wade* had been driving? Could that be? Was Lucas truly innocent?

No. Lucas wasn't the martyr type. He would never have confessed. Why would he? To protect Wade's reputation? Hardly. Jake might have turned Wade into some larger-than-life hero in his mind, but Claire knew better. Wade McRoyan was a selfish, even cruel person, well on his way to becoming a serious drunk.

"I have to think," Claire said aloud, squeezing her head with both hands.

She followed the path around the side of the house, through the rosebushes and flowery shrubs in the front yard. She glanced at her watch. Six twenty-five. Zoey would be on the six-thirty ferry, arriving at ten till seven. She needed to see Benjamin before that. Find out just what was going on in his head.

And then, Jake.

She walked quickly through the center of town, just five minutes to Benjamin's house. She rapped at his window, letting him know she was there. Mr. Passmore often took a nap in the early evening.

She waited by the front door until Benjamin came and let her in. She followed him to his room. Here in his own home he moved with all the ease and assurance of a sighted person.

She gave him a little kiss, just brushing his lips.

"I didn't expect you," Benjamin said, sitting down on his bed.

"I didn't know I had to make an appointment," Claire said, trying to sound pleasant and unhurried. Inside she was boiling with impatience. It was strange. She wasn't an impatient person.

"Of course you don't," Benjamin said. "Why don't you come here and give me a real kiss?"

She felt anger flare. He was so smug, so sure he was smarter than everyone else around him, with his so clever upside-down posters, his eerie impersonation of a sighted person, his terrible concentration on everything and everyone around him. What a relief it was to be with someone like Jake. Jake was so easy to be with, so straightforward.

"You know, Benjamin," Claire began, hearing the false notes in her own voice, "lately, with Lucas coming back and all, I've been thinking a lot about what happened. The accident, I mean."

There it was: the hint of a smug grin, quickly repressed but not quickly enough.

"Uh-huh," he said, drawing out the last syllable to ironic extreme.

"You know I've never been able to remember that whole thing."

He waited for her, silent. She fidgeted, sticking her fingers into the pot of aromatic herbs hanging in front of his window, and looking down the street, half-expecting to see Zoey come walking up. "I mean, Lucas pleaded guilty, didn't he?" She yanked her hands back to her sides. Amazing. She was trembling. Her voice was shaky. He couldn't help but hear it.

"Yes, he did," Benjamin agreed.

"So he must have been driving, right?" Claire demanded.

Now Benjamin let his slow, infuriating grin spread across his face. "Ah. So. It's always interesting to watch how long it takes for information to travel across this island. But I was sure you'd already heard about my speculations."

"I haven't heard anything," Claire snapped, not really expecting him to believe her. "What bull are you spreading around? That's all I want to know."

"You're ready to climb a wall," he said wonderingly. "I don't think I've ever seen you like this before."

"I don't like lies and rumors, that's all," Claire said. "If Lucas confessed, why are you going around trying to get everyone to believe Wade was driving that car? Why are you trying to help Lucas?"

To her amazement, Benjamin actually laughed. "I'll be damned, Claire. You really

234

don't remember, do you?" He shook his head. In a low, kind voice he said, "Poor Claire. I was too cynical; I'm sorry. I assumed from the way you were acting, the frantic way you were attacking Lucas, that weird offer from your dad . . . But you actually don't remember."

"What the hell are you talking about, Benjamin? Why don't you just wipe that smug look off your face and spit it out?"

Benjamin stood up and crossed to her. He fumbled for and found her, holding her by the shoulders, his face now sincerely sad. "I'll always stand by you, Claire. I want you to know that. Whatever you decide. Not because your dad tried to bribe me."

Claire pushed him away violently. He fell back onto his bed. "You're scaring me!" she shouted.

You're scaring me!

She felt as if a bolt of electricity had shot up her spine. She reached for the wall, pressing her palm against it, trying to regain her balance in a spinning room.

Stop it. Pull over. You're scaring me.

"It's coming back, isn't it?" Benjamin asked softly.

"No!" Claire cried.

"It wasn't Lucas driving," Benjamin said, the words tumbling out at top speed. "He was the only one who was uninjured. He was in the backseat, wasn't he?"

"I have to get out of here," Claire said. "I—I have to . . . I—" She reeled toward the door.

"Claire, wait!" Benjamin cried.

Claire ran.

BENJAMIN

I had wondered from the start, from the first few moments after the initial shock of the news had worn off.

Maybe it's because I can't see. Sight is very convincing. When you see something, you don't doubt that it's true. You see something, ~~instnalty~~ instantly you know what it is, and you know it to be real, absolutely, with utter confidence. It doesn't take a lot of interpretation. You don't spend much time guessing.

Hearing, smell, ~~tuoch~~ touch are all so much less certain. And when you have to rely on those uncertain senses, when you have to rely on senses that you are trained to believe are unreliable, you find certainty very much harder to achieve.

I won't say being blind has made me suspicious; that would be the wrong word. But where sighted people are in the habit of simply accepting what seems obvious, I'm in the habit of guessing, reasoning, imagining.

So when all my sighted friends learned that Wade McRoyan had ~~sied~~ died in a car with Lucas and Claire, and when they had *seen* the body, and *seen* Claire's injuries, and *seen* the car crumpled around that tree trunk, those sights became all-important.

Whereas I could only imagine. I had to imagine a car. And imagine three people sitting in it. You see, I had to place them there in my imagination, and at that point the question arose: Who was in the backseat?

One dead. One injured. One uninjured.

Wade. Claire. Lucas.

I couldn't be sure at that point who *was* driving the car, but I was pretty certain who was not.

And then, Lucas confessed. And Claire couldn't remember.

I figured I was wrong. I didn't guess the full truth until Lucas came back and I saw how Claire reacted.

I don't know how much she ~~rememm-bared~~ remembered over time, or half-remembered, or suspected. She's a person who will act on intuition, and I guess that's what she did. I like to think if she had known the truth two years ago, she'd have told it. Claire is a decent person underneath all her compulsive manipulation. If she'd remembered the truth back then, she never would have let Lucas pay the price he did.

I have to ~~beleive~~ believe that. It's the only way I can keep on loving her.

Eighteen

"Look, the important thing is you have to act like you just happened to be passing by," Nina said for the dozenth time.

Aisha rolled her eyes. Like Nina was the person to be giving lectures on how to be discreet. Nina, who had spilled the news about Zoey and Lucas to her within fifteen minutes of having heard it.

Now they were standing around the dock, practicing so they'd look casual when the ferry came in with Zoey and Lucas aboard. Aisha was supposed to pretend she had just been passing by and *Oh, there's Nina, I'll go over and say hi, and oh, there's Zoey on the ferry. What a major coincidence!*

"I'll be totally cool, all right? I mean, I'm not personally quite as worked up over this as you are."

"Zoey and Lucas?" Nina said incredulously. "You think that's no big deal?"

"Well, it's big, I mean as far as gossip and so

239

on, but I don't think it will be a life-altering experience for me." She looked at her watch, then glanced out toward the setting sun. "There's the *Minnow*."

"Okay, now run away."

"Away where?"

"I don't know. Jeez, Aisha, do I have to think of everything?"

"This is your particular insanity, Nina," Aisha said.

"Run over to Passmores'. If she sees you there, you'll just say you went in for a Coke."

"Should we synchronize our watches?" Aisha asked. "That's what they do in the spy movies."

"Would you rather I just hadn't told you?" Nina asked.

Aisha considered that question as she trotted across the parking area to Passmores'. There were two tables filled in the outdoor seating area, and the sound of more diners inside.

Aisha lurked by the alleyway, self-consciously keeping her head down as the ferry chugged across the harbor.

So, Zoey was fooling around with Lucas. It was juicy, no question about it. Stupid, too, probably. But then, Zoey did have this suppressed crazy streak deep down inside that you didn't really notice till you'd known her awhile. Plus, she was hopelessly, pathetically romantic, which was the kind of character trait that got people into trouble. Much better to be rational.

It was one thing to look at a guy and think, Hey, not bad. But that didn't mean you acted on it. Otherwise, you'd constantly be getting led around one way or another, a prisoner of whatever chance happened to bring a good-looking guy your way.

The ferry whistle split the calm night. None of the diners at the café flinched or jumped, which showed that they were locals. Aisha looked at them more closely. Pastor what-was-his-name and his wife. And the two gay guys who had the house on Pond Road.

Zoey and Lucas. Definitely running counter to peer pressure on that one. Not that peer pressure should be your guide. If it were, well, she'd be going out with Christopher, wouldn't she?

She flashed on an image of him, tight, very tight bike shorts, running down the field, keeping the ball just ahead of him, his cute little . . . But then, that was exactly the point. Zoey was the kind of person who'd let that get to her. Aisha was not. She could separate out the fact that he was good-looking and not be influenced in the slightest. And she could ignore everyone's expectations.

Aisha nodded, feeling content.

Besides, Nina didn't have a boyfriend, either. Lots of girls didn't have boyfriends.

"Order up." She heard the familiar voice close at hand, but muffled. She jumped around and stared down the alley. "Come on, pick up, it's getting cold."

Of course. Christopher cooked at Passmores'. It was one of his seemingly endless profusion of jobs. The kitchen door was just down the alleyway.

Aisha glanced anxiously toward the ferry. It was nosing into the dock, but it would take four more minutes before they tied it off and lowered the gangplank.

She sidled down the alley, stepping carefully so as not to make a noise. Hot, moist, aromatic air blasted from the doorway, along with the crash of aluminum pots and the roar of a dishwasher.

"You need drawn butter with that," Christopher said.

Aisha flattened herself against the brick wall and peered around the corner. The kitchen was blazingly bright, fluorescence gleaming off stainless steel. Christopher was only a few feet away, his back to her as he placed a green garnish on a plate of fish.

He was wearing a white apron over cutoff shorts and a blue T-shirt. On his head he had a baseball cap turned backward.

He moved from the range to the broiler, shaking a frying pan here, lifting a plate there, sailing a steak through the air to land on the grill. It was almost graceful. Almost like a dance of some sort, and he did it well.

He bent over at the waist, reaching into a low refrigerator, and pulled out a cake, sliced it, spooned strawberries over it, and, with a flourish, sprayed a mound of whipped cream on top.

"Here," he said, turning very suddenly to face her.

Aisha leapt back, but it was too late. He leaned out of the door and handed the strawberry shortcake to her, producing a clean spoon from the pocket of his apron.

"I . . . I . . ." she said.

"You are hungry, aren't you?" he asked smugly. "I mean, that is why you came sneaking down the alleyway, right? You wanted something to eat? Surely it wasn't to see little old me."

"I just happened to be here."

"I see. On your way to—" He made a point of turning his head slowly. "On your way to the brick wall at the end of the alley."

243

"I'm waiting for someone," Aisha said furiously.

"Uh-huh. I know you are, but I'm working right now, Aisha." He grabbed her hand and thrust the dish into it. "Try this, it may satisfy at least some of your craving." He winked outrageously and disappeared back into his kitchen.

Aisha threw the dish hard against the bricks. "Why can't I get rid of you?"

He leaned back through the doorway, looking serious and a little angry. "If you really want to be rid of me, you can," he said. "I'll never speak to you again, never look at you, put you out of my mind permanently. If that's what you really, truly want. You have three seconds to say *Get out of my life*."

"I, uh, I—" she stammered.

"One."

"Look—"

"Two."

"Christopher!"

"Three." He nodded cockily. "Didn't think so."

The creep, Aisha thought grumpily.

Claire walked for several hours, through the narrow, familiar streets of North Harbor, along the breakwater, in the sand on Town Beach. She sat on a bench in the circle for a while, till the bells from the steeple rang eight and roused her from her thoughts.

She knew she should go home, but she knew she couldn't. Not yet.

Inevitably her feet found Coast Road, and she turned south. It was a mile, more, till the houses, some bright, some shuttered and empty, thinned out, leaving her with only the crashing surf for company. The last of the widely spaced streetlights fell behind, and now only the milky light of a startlingly bright moon showed her the way. It was another half-mile to the intersection with Pond Road, down which she saw more homes, more light, but she plunged on into lonely darkness.

In two years she had not returned to the spot, and she wondered if she would know it when she got there.

But then a chill breeze raised goose bumps on her arms and shoulders. Her steps faltered on the sand-blown blacktop.

Yes. This was the place. The moon's diffuse glow seemed to cast a spotlight on the vast white scar, the tree trunk naked, its bark ripped away long ago.

She stood there, staring, not really thinking, just letting her mind go blank. And then, after a while, she realized she was crying.

*　　　*　　　*

"Zoey, how *could* you?"

They sat in the middle of the circle, Zoey lying back on the grass, Aisha with legs and arms crossed sitting on the bench, Nina pacing back and forth, chewing her unlit Lucky Strike. The sun had set, plunging North Harbor into darkness softened by a dusky moon overhead.

Zoey had met the two of them at the dock, instantly realizing that despite their lame attempt to make it look like a coincidence, Nina had, of course, told Aisha everything.

When he'd seen them, Lucas had squeezed her hand and prudently disappeared into the disembarking crowd.

"You don't understand," Zoey said, trying to calm her heart, trying to keep her head from spinning. "It's like—it's like you're happy with regular old store ice cream until you discover Ben and Jerry's."

Aisha rolled her eyes toward Nina. "Look," she said, leaning forward, "I think you're kind of missing the point a little, Zoey. I mean, sure, right now all you see is the good stuff with Lucas—"

"—whatever that might be," Nina interjected.

"But you can't ruin your life just because some guy gives you a case of heaving bosom."

"I know," Zoey said dreamily.

"Do you realize what this will do to everyone?" Aisha asked. "We've always gotten along all right, the six of us. You, me, Nina, Claire . . . most of the time, Benjamin, Jake. We're a group, we're buds."

"We're all stuck with each other, trapped together like rats in a cage," Nina said. "Every morning we're on the ferry together, every evening the same thing. In between we go to the same school and live so close together that you could just about throw a baseball from your house to anyone else's house."

"I know," Zoey said, more seriously this time. She sat up and wrapped her arms around her knees. She took a deep breath and closed her eyes. "I know this will really hurt Jake."

"It's not just that," Nina said. "I don't care if Jake gets hurt. It's that, I mean, we won't be a group anymore."

"You hate being part of a group, Nina," Zoey pointed out. "You're the raging nonconformist here."

"I know, but still, I need a group to rebel against."

"It will be like civil war around here," Aisha said glumly. "You and Lucas on one side, Jake and Claire on the other. We won't be together anymore. Don't try to fool yourself, Zoey. This isn't just like you're seeing another guy; it's like you've decided to go steady with Satan or something and you're trying to convince yourself that everyone will accept him eventually."

"Really, Zo," Nina said.

"So what am I supposed to do?" Zoey shouted in sudden exasperation. "You want me just to give Lucas up because it will keep the group together?"

"Sounds kind of unromantic when you put it that way," Nina said.

"Look, romance is not the only thing in the world," Aisha said. "People do stupid things for love. How about the Trojan War? Paris and Helen go at it and Agamemnon ends up being chopped up by his wife while he's taking a bath."

"Excuse me?" Nina said. "Could we stick to reality here?"

"I can't stop feeling something because it's inconvenient," Zoey said.

"Of course you can. I do it all the time," Aisha argued.

"You're right, though," Zoey went on, talking almost to herself. "Things won't be the same, will they? It's like we've all been going along in this pleasant little dream and I'm going to screw it up."

"Forget about us," Nina said, suddenly serious. "What about you, Zo? You won't be part of

Zoey and Jake anymore. You won't be the couple everyone looks up to. Barbie and Ken. You'll be part of Zoey and Lucas.

"It's your decision, Zo," Nina went on. She looked at her friend, for once without a hint of irony in her eyes. "Only it's maybe bigger than you think."

Claire found her father in his study, a dark-paneled room lined with expensively bound books and lit from green-shaded lamps. He was in a deep leather wing chair, smoking a cigar, sipping a glass of scotch, and reading through a sheaf of official-looking papers with a detached look.

"Daddy," she said.

"Oh, hi there, honey. Where've you been?"

Claire came into the room and sank into a chair opposite him. She tried to meet his eyes, but looked down at the carpet instead. It took a while to put the words together. "How did you get Lucas to do it?"

"What?" His voice was confused. He pulled the cigar from his mouth and set the glass on a table. "What was that?"

"How did you get Lucas to confess that he was driving the car?"

"Me?" Her father made an effort at a smile.

"Daddy, I remember," Claire said in a choked voice. "It wasn't Lucas."

249

"I don't know . . . what are you—"

"Lucas wasn't driving the car," Claire said flatly. "He was in the backseat. He was complaining, he was saying we were all too damned drunk to be driving and we should walk back into town. He was making a joke out of it. *Stop it. Pull over. You're scaring me.* He was joking, but he was serious."

Her father's confused look vanished. "I think you're just imagining things, honey. I know how much you've wanted to remember—"

"Have I?" Claire snapped. "How hard have I tried?"

"It's not your fault. You had a concussion, for God's sake."

"He wasn't hurt, Lucas wasn't hurt; Benjamin's right. Because he was in the backseat. He was in the back yelling that we should pull over and not try to drive."

"Look, memory's a tricky thing—"

"But he confessed. Why? To protect Wade? Why? He didn't care about Wade. No. He cared about me, though. He was in love with me."

"Love," her father snorted.

"Tell me the truth, Daddy," Claire begged. "It wasn't Lucas driving."

"Wade, then," her father said. "Maybe you're right. Maybe it was Wade."

Claire laughed bitterly. "It was me. It was

me!" Her voice broke and she buried her face in her hands. "I was driving the car. Me."

For a long while, neither of them spoke. Then her father, in a dull monotone, said, "There was no conclusive evidence."

"Until now. Now I remember."

And not before? Or had the truth always been there, just below the surface of her dreams? Why else had she been so frightened when Lucas reappeared? Why else had it been so important to get rid of him? Had she sensed somehow that his coming would prod her guilty memory?

Fear. That's what she had felt, learning he was back. Unreasoning fear. She'd done her best to shut him out. And in her fear she'd turned away from Benjamin, probing, suspicious Benjamin, and felt herself drawn to Jake. Jake would be her ally against the common foe. Safe, dependable Jake.

"Old Officer Talbot, hell, you know they send the old cops over here to take it easy till retirement," her father said, gazing at her with unfocused eyes. "He'd been at a desk since the sixties, hadn't investigated anything for years. But he was bound and determined, it was a crime, dammit, someone had to pay."

"It should have been me," Claire whispered.

"Everyone knew the Cabral kid had been in

trouble before. What was it to him? He'd have ended up in jail sooner or later."

"Oh, God."

"At first it was Lucas's own idea, do what he must have figured was the manly thing: protect his girlfriend by taking the rap for her. For you." Her father nodded. "It was probably the only really gutsy thing he'd ever done. But I was worried sooner or later someone would think about it: Why was he the only one not hurt? The driver's side of that car was crushed like a beer can. Only someone small could have been behind that wheel and survived. The McRoyan kid was six three. Lucas Cabral was smaller, but he'd at least have been badly hurt, not untouched." For the first time he met her gaze. "No. I couldn't be sure it was you driving, sweetheart, but it was most likely, and if I could figure it out, so could someone else."

"I remember now," Claire said in a faraway voice. "The door was popped open by the impact and Lucas had to get my seat to recline before he could get me out. I could barely breathe from the wheel pressing against me."

"I told Lucas I thought he was taking it like a man, confessing to what he'd done." Her father hung his head. "I told him I hoped he would have the guts to stick to his story. We never really admitted out loud that he was innocent. He never claimed he was, and I really didn't want to know for sure that he was." He closed his eyes and sighed profoundly. "Still, we reached an agreement. His father's business had been slipping for a while, lots of problems with the boat, prices for lobster were at rock bottom. Cabral was a razor's edge away from losing his boat altogether. I told Lucas I'd be able to help with that."

"Oh, God, Daddy," Claire whispered.

"I didn't think he'd go to jail," her father said sadly. "Everyone figured he'd just get a slap on the wrist, being a juvenile and all. You have to believe that. I didn't think . . . And it was easy to see how shaken up he was when the judge handed down the sentence. But he took that, too, and just as they were leading him out of the courtroom he said to me, 'Don't worry, Mr. Geiger. I keep my promises.'"

"All this time," Claire whispered. "He thinks I know. He thinks I've let this happen to him, that I just abandoned him. It's sickening. I feel like throwing up."

Her father's gaze was steely. "I do whatever I have to to protect you. Whatever. Even perjury."

"Perjury?" she asked, uncomprehending.

"That's what they'd call it, I imagine: subornation of perjury. If you ever told anyone what we've just discussed, I might even wind up in jail myself."

"He went to jail to protect me, and to save his father," Claire whispered.

Her father smiled bitterly. "People do all sorts of things to protect the ones they love."

Claire felt the weight of his words settle on her. Yes, people did all sorts of things to protect the ones they loved.

And now, it would be her turn.

"You know I love you, honey," her father said.

"I love you, too, Daddy."

The List

Jake	Lucas
-Known him for years	~~Feel like I~~ Feel like I ~~Barely~~ Know him <u>well</u>
-Great body	-Okay body
-Like his mom	-His dad is a little intense
-Very good Kisser	-~~?~~ Exellent Kisser ~~Maybe~~
-Never got anyone Killed	-~~Probably~~ got someone Killed He paid for it, though
-Everyone likes him but Nina	-No one likes him ~~but~~ <u>me</u>
-Thinks he's going to marry me	-Says he thought of me a lot
-Getting Kind of gropey	-Hasn't seen a girl in 2 years
-Friend as well as boyfriend	-Neither ????? Makes me feel <u>amazing</u>
-Makes me feel safe	-~~Makes me feel~~
-Excellent chest	-Possible tattoo?
-Don't like his hair	-Nice hair

Zoey stared thoughtfully at the list. Things had definitely improved for Lucas, she realized. Definite, major improvement. But when she'd made the first list, she hadn't really known Lucas, not like she did now.

She snapped off the little lamp over her desk and gazed out the window. The moon was so bright, it must be full. The cobblestones were painted silver; the shadows were soft and benign.

She craned her neck out of the small window to try to get a glimpse of the Cabrals' deck. Too bad her window didn't face the other way. Then maybe she could look up at him, and he'd be able to see her down below if he stepped out onto his balcony.

Maybe he was already asleep, possibly even dreaming of her. Was he a guy who would dream? Probably. He was thoughtful and intelligent and romantic, even though he tried to hide it under typical male toughness.

Yes, he certainly dreamed. And if he did dream, why not of her? She was certain she would dream of him. Oh, definitely; in fact, it was the best reason ever for going to sleep early.

At least in their dreams they wouldn't have to worry about how Jake would react—no guilt, no feeling that you were betraying someone you thought you loved.

And in their dreams there would be no

Claire, no Nina shaking her head like she had, saying, Jeez, Zoey, do you really want to do this? No Aisha making snide remarks about how naive you were. No group to be split for the first time ever into angry camps.

She pushed her chair back impatiently and began pacing the room. It was the island. It was too small, too intimate. Anywhere would be better. In a big city who would even notice whom she went out with?

Was he still awake? Probably; it was early still. Too early for dreams, but still, he might be thinking of her, right now, this very minute, only a few dozen feet away.

She lay back on her bed. Was he lying on his bed?

She closed her eyes and pictured him, the look in his eyes when they had separated after that first earth-shattering kiss. Was he remembering that same moment, right now, lying on his bed?

She jumped up, impatient, agitated, sleep an absolute impossibility. She would never fall asleep, not this night. Not the way she felt, her mind racing, her insides jittery, her limbs rattling with too much energy.

Had she felt like this with Jake? *Honestly,* she scolded herself, *did you ever feel this way with Jake?*

No. Yes, sort of, in a way. But not this way, not this precise way.

Was she falling in love with Lucas?

What a ridiculous thing to think. They'd only spent one afternoon together. And that time on the breakwater. And when he had met her at the breakfast table.

Was that enough?

She opened the door to her room stealthily and crept to the guest room. It was at the back of the house, with windows that looked up toward his.

Kneeling and looking up, she could just see the Cabral house. The lights were off. Of course, those were the lights in his parents' room, not his.

Suddenly a delicious thrill went through her. She was going to go and see. She had to know if he was awake or asleep.

She tiptoed back to her room and quickly put on her sneakers. With the Boston Bruins nightshirt, a slightly unfashionable outfit.

Walking at a snail's pace, she descended the stairs, reaching far to skip the one that squeaked. Then it was out the front door into the night.

The cool night air surprised her, blowing through and under her shirt. She felt wonderfully dangerous, creeping around her house, finding the narrow path through the bushes.

She climbed carefully, fell and scuffed her bare knees on the dirt, and almost dissolved in nervous giggles. This was basically a pretty dorky thing to be doing at nearly midnight. Mr. Cabral would probably wake up and think she was a burglar.

She reached the top, panting a little from exertion and excitement, and made her silent way around to the front of his house. There was a single window on the second floor, dormered like hers. The light was off.

So, he was in his bed. Asleep and dreaming, or awake, unable to sleep for thinking of her.

Or neither, some dark, unromantic corner of her mind suggested.

"Zoey?"

"Ahhhh!"

"Shh," Lucas said, clapping his hand over her mouth. When she was quiet he removed his hand, and smothered her giggles with his lips. She melted into his arms, letting her hands travel down his back and making the shocking discovery that he wore no shirt.

He pulled away, then kissed her again, a kiss that lasted so long she was sure the moon would have set and the sun come up by the time they drew apart again.

His eyes glittered darkly, so near she might

fall into them and never find her way out again.

"I . . . I just wanted to see if your light was on," Zoey admitted. Would he think she was an idiot, prowling around in the dark on such a ridiculous mission?

He nodded. "I couldn't sleep either. I was thinking of you."

"Me too. I mean, of you."

He held her close, but now Zoey sensed a heaviness, a sadness in him that made him cling all the harder.

"What's wrong?" she asked, craning back to look into his downturned face.

He sighed. "I, uh, I had a fight with my father," he said.

"Was it bad?"

He nodded and pulled away, withdrawing his touch. "He wants me gone," Lucas said in a flat, monotone voice. "He's arranged with my grandfather for me to go there, until I can graduate."

Zoey felt her heart stop. "Your grandfather?"

"Yeah. My grandfather who lives in Texas." He clenched his fists and turned away.

Zoey flew to him, wrapping her arms around him, pressing her cheek against his back. "You have to talk to him, make him change his mind!"

"My father's never changed his mind about

anything," Lucas said bitterly. "A few weeks from now—"

"No, Lucas, no," Zoey said desperately. "We'll figure something out; you can't . . . I can't . . ."

"Just kiss me again, Zoey," he said. "When you kiss me, nothing bad can happen."

They kissed in the moonlight, desperate with longing, afraid, their tears mingling, and slowly, slowly, the rest of the world faded away, leaving them perfectly alone together.

About the Author

After Katherine Applegate graduated from college, she spent time waiting tables, typing (badly), watering plants, wandering randomly from one place to the next with her boyfriend, and just generally wasting her time. When she grew sufficiently tired of performing brain-dead minimum-wage work, she decided it was time to become a famous writer. Anyway, a writer. Writing proved to be an ideal career choice, as it involved neither physical exertion nor uncomfortable clothing and required no social skills.

Ms. Applegate has written forty books under her own name and a variety of pseudonyms. She has no children, is active in no organizations, and has never been invited to address a joint session of Congress. She does, however, have an evil, foot-biting cat named Dick, and she still enjoys wandering randomly from one place to the next with her boyfriend.

So you think you know about love. . . .

Do you prefer change to stability? Uncertain first kisses to comfortably familiar nuzzles? Slick new motorcycles to battered bikes built for two? Are "excitement" and "long-term relationship" mutually exclusive terms? Take this quiz and discover how you feel about falling in love, being in love, and bidding love farewell.

1. *Your best friend is going on a first date with a guy she just met. Having been in a relationship for two years, you:*
   a. pity her for having to cover the usual first date basics: her favorite subject in school, her favorite movie, her favorite music and other I-could-care-less-but-I-have-to-make-conversation conversation.
   b. go into a jealous rage wherein you get a new haircut, reorganize your bedroom, and flirt with the bus driver, your guidance counselor, and your family's accountant.
   c. tell her to have fun and offer to lend her your striped mini-skirt, which looks great on her.

2. *If love were food, it would be:*
   a. brown rice and lentils. Fat-free, cholesterol-free, yet a complete protein nonetheless. (Hint: chopped spinach contributes iron.)
   b. mushroom lasagna, Caesar salad, a little garlic bread. All the right vitamins, just enough spice.
   c. a chocolate chocolate-chip ice-cream sundae with

whipped cream, peanuts, walnuts, *and* pecans. It'll melt within minutes, but it's creamy dreamy while it lasts.

3. *While your boyfriend is away for the weekend, you and your friends go dancing. When the guy you've been dancing with asks you to go for some fresh air, you:*
   a. explain politely that you're already seeing someone so you don't think a walk is a particularly good idea.
   b. say, why not? This could be interesting . . .
   c. shriek in horror that he would dare try to come between you and your boyfriend.

4. *You're out with your boyfriend of two years, and the object of your lust since grade school walks by and winks at you. You:*
   a. excuse yourself to the ladies room, follow him to a remote corner, and slip your number into his hand.
   b. ignore him. You're lucky to be with a guy who *really* appreciates you.
   c. grab your boyfriend and give him a gigantic kiss to show the stupid flirt that he's way too late.

5. *Your boyfriend has to go out of town for Valentine's Day. Your friends think it would be fun if all of you participated in the Dating Game that your school has organized. In response you:*

a. decide to ham it up with phony giggles and eye-lash batting. It'll be a fun, goofy way to spend the holiday.
b. spend hours deliberating over what you'll wear for the occasion and start practicing all the ways you'll flirt with Bachelors #1, #2, and/or #3.
c. say you already *have* plans for Valentine's Day, thank you very much. What were they thinking? You've planned a romantic evening at home with your boyfriend's photograph.

6. *Your best male friend since kindergarten confesses that he has a crush on you and asks you out. This is most definitely:*
a. confusing. Maybe you'll try holding his hand for a few minutes and see what happens.
b. fate. Once you built Lego houses and raised an ant farm with this guy; soon you'll build a country cottage and raise children and a litter of German shepherds with him.
c. out of the question. How could you go out with someone you'd seen throw a tantrum over a spilled chocolate milk shake?

7. *Your boyfriend's family is moving out-of-state. He wants to have a long-distance relationship. You:*
a. sob, beat your fists against the wall, and vow to speak with him every evening and to visit him every weekend.
b. call up the guy who sits in front of you in

Spanish class and has such nice curly hair. You're a soon-to-be-free woman.

c. give it a shot, but if someone at home should just so happen to sweep you off your feet, don't say, "Why, no, I couldn't possibly. . . ."

8. *After your first fight with your boyfriend, you:*

a. take a long, hot bath. By your next fight this will be a distant memory. And you'll be even better at making up.

b. split. Who needs this?

c. throw yourself at his feet, say that you'll never ever argue with him again and make him swear the same. In the future, you take out all your anger on your little brother.

Scoring

1) a=2; b=0; c=1
2) a=2; b=1; c=0
3) a=1; b=0; c=2
4) a=0; b=1; c=2
5) a=1; b=0; c=2
6) a=1; b=2; c=0
7) a=2; b=0; c=1
8) a=1; b=0; c=2

16-12: Well, you're into loyalty and commitment, that's for sure. So much so, in fact, that you tend to lose sight of such things as friends, schoolwork, your individual identity. . . . And what's more, in your single-minded passion, you could end up driving everyone away, including your beloved. Oops. Sure, it's nice to love the one you're with, but you might want to remind yourself that there's a whole world outside your little love bubble.

11-6: Your love is so perfectly balanced between sparks and security, it's almost scary. You can be as mushy gushy as anyone, but you're realistic enough to know when it's time to move on or simply to tone down the frills. How on earth do you manage it?

5-0: Restless much? The good news is that you're open to change and know how to get out of a bad thing. The bad news is you're *always* looking for a new thing, even when you're in a good thing. Could be that by turning away from a familiar love at every opportunity you're actually cheating yourself. Long-term doesn't have to mean boring. And it *is* possible to fall in love with the same person more than once.

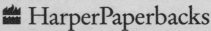